THE GRASS WIDOW

LORI BEASLEY BRADLEY

Copyright (C) 2017 Lori Beasley Bradley

Layout design and Copyright (C) 2021 by Next Chapter

Published 2021 by Next Chapter

Edited by Fading Street Services

Cover art by CoverMint

Back cover texture by David M. Schrader, used under license from Shutterstock.com

Mass Market Paperback Edition

This book is a work of fiction. Names, characters, places, and incidents are the product of the author's imagination or are used fictitiously. Any resemblance to actual events, locales, or persons, living or dead, is purely coincidental.

All rights reserved. No part of this book may be reproduced or transmitted in any form or by any means, electronic or mechanical, including photocopying, recording, or by any information storage and retrieval system, without the author's permission.

CHAPTER 1
CALLIE'S FALL

What, in the name of God, did I do to deserve this shame and humiliation?

Callie Jamison sat stiff-backed, wearing her best black suit and bonnet, her mourning garb. She brushed aside tears of rage and shame. She sat in her husband's one-horse buggy, trotting down Front Street in Ellsworth, Kansas. They were coming from the courthouse on the sunny June morning where a judge had just dissolved her ten-year marriage to Evan Jamison.

I was a good wife.

Tears of shame stained Callie's tanned cheek, and she refused to look at Evan. How could he have done this to her? She was now a divorced woman—a grass widow. How would she ever bear the shame and ridicule? Divorced women were to be shunned.

"Here you go, Callie," Evan sneered as he brought the buggy to a halt in front of The Ellsworth House, "your new home."

"You can't be serious," Callie gasped as she stared up at the three-story wood-framed building with Ellsworth House stenciled in gold on the big front window. "I can't stay in this place it's … it's disreputable."

"The judge said I had to pay for your room and board in a suitable residence," Evan sneered. "You're a disreputable woman now, Callie, so this is plenty suitable for you as far as I can reckon." Evan began to chuckle as he lifted her three carpet bags from the back of the buggy.

"Come on, woman," Evan snapped as he carried her bags toward the door of the boarding house, "I don't have all day. I've got a ranch to run."

And I suppose you're going to be moving that little girl into my house as soon as you can.

Evan had made no secret of his affair with Polly Hardin, the nineteen-year-old daughter of a neighbor and one of Callie's former students at the school, where she'd taught Ellsworth's children for the last seven years.

Callie took a deep breath, hitched up her skirts and stepped down from the buggy. A warm, dry breeze blew a loose strand of auburn hair into her tear-filled blue eyes and Callie brushed it back into place with her gloved hand. She held her head high, straightened her jacket, and stepped up onto the dusty boardwalk.

She struggled to put one foot in front of the other as she followed Evan into the gaudy lobby of the town boarding house, and brothel if the rumors were correct. Young women in loose-fitting, lacy dressing gowns sat on settees covered in red velvet upholstery. Callie needed no more evidence to know the rumors were correct. The Ellsworth House was, indeed, a brothel.

I'm going to petition the judge. This is anything but suitable for a schoolteacher and churchgoing woman. Evan can't possibly be serious.

"What can I do for you folks?" the tall scar-faced man behind the counter asked, eyeing the bags Evan carried and Callie. The man's deep-set dark eyes sent a shiver down Callie's spine as he stood leering down at her.

"Do you have that room ready I talked to you about, Caine?" Evan asked with a satisfied grin at Callie.

"I know you wanted her on the third floor," Matthew Caine said with his eyes on Callie. He licked his thin lips and grinned, "but I've had to put her downstairs with the girls until something opens up there. I have a full house just now."

"Ain't she a bit old to be down with us, Matt?" one of the young women called out. "She looks to be as old as my ma, and just as prudish with her high collar and pinned up hair under that matron's bonnet." The other women laughed, and Callie felt her cheeks flush with embarrassment as her eyes stung with fresh tears.

I'm going to petition that judge if I must crawl to the courthouse on my knees. I can't stay in this horrid place with these women.

"I don't care where the hell you put her," Evan snapped and dropped Callie's bags on the polished wood floor. "She's no never-mind of mine now." He threw his hands into the air, turned, and stormed out of the lobby.

"Well, ain't he a sweetheart," one of the young women hissed as she came to stand beside Callie. "Where do you want her, Matt?" she asked the tall man. "Ruthie's old room?"

The tall man nodded without taking his eyes off Callie's bosoms.

I'd swear he's measuring me for a dress.

"Come on, honey," the girl said and bent to pick

up two of Callie's discarded bags, "I'll show ya to your room."

Callie stooped, picked up her other bag, and followed the slender redhead past the counter and down a narrow, dark hall papered with the same gaudy flocked wallpaper as the lobby.

"We girls use these rooms," the girl explained, "because there's a door to the outside at the end of the hall so our clients don't have to leave through the lobby," she said pointing to a hazy light at the far end of the hall, "and so that nosy fuck, Caine, don't know our comings and goings," she added as she opened a door near the lobby end of the hall.

"There's no key?" Callie asked as she flinched at the young woman's use of the vulgarity, wide-eyed and appalled.

The redhead carried Callie's bags into a room where a big brass-framed bed sat as the central feature and a tall wardrobe with a cracked oval mirror in one door stood on the opposite wall. She saw a washstand with an enameled pitcher and bowl. A matching chamber pot sat on the floor beside the bed. A small vanity stood beside the window with an oval mirror on the wall above it. The room smelled as though the former resident had left the chamber pot full upon departing and nobody had bothered to empty it.

"My name is Maisie," the girl said, offering her petite, freckled hand, "but most of the girls just call me Ruby for my hair."

"Which do you prefer?" Callie asked and took the girl's warm hand.

Maisie gave her a perplexed look as if nobody had ever asked the question before. "Ma and my granny always called me Mae," the girl whispered, "You can call me Mae if you want."

"I'm Callie," she said as she shook Mae's hand. "Thanks for the help with the bags, Mae."

"No, bother," the pretty girl said with a grin that pushed the freckled balls of her cheeks up beneath her bright, green eyes. "Matt is a terrible bother," she said, "and a lazy ass. He sends us clients, takes the pay, and keeps more than his ten percent, we're all fairly certain," Mae said with narrowed eyes. "Be careful of him," she warned. "I don't like the way he was ogling ya out there."

At least I'm not the only one who noticed.

"You'll have to get your own water from the pump out back and carry your chamber pot to the outhouse. It's out back too, but you can get to it easy from the door at the end of the hall."

Her eyes darted around the room and stopped at the bed with its thin ticking mattress without a pillow. "You'll have to supply your own bedding, I'm afraid," Mae sighed. "Most of us carry ours with us in our trunks as we travel from town to town, but you can get new at the mercantile down the street."

"Thanks," Callie said with a frown. She hadn't considered the need for bedding when she'd hurriedly packed her things that morning. She'd assumed Evan would take her to the hotel and not drop her into this whorehouse.

Callie had been sure of what the outcome at the courthouse would be, however. Evan and Judge Sterling were poker-buddies and Callie had known the man would grant Evan the divorce he wanted.

"Do you have money?" the girl asked meekly. "If you don't, I can front you a few dollars until you do."

"I have a little," Callie said with a weak grin, "but thank you, kindly for the offer."

"It's not easy being a woman on your own," Mae sighed. "You have to pay for everything. Most of us take our meals at the Flat Iron Café across the street. Old man Jenkins trades off meals for a suck in the kitchen every now and again when his wife ain't there," she said with her cheeks turning red.

Callie knew Hiram Jenkins and grinned. "I think I can afford the few cents for a meal."

"Oh," the girl added as she went to the door, "here's your key," she said, taking the key from the lock, and handing it to Callie. "We all keep ours with us," Mae added with a shake of her curly red head. "We never leave them with Caine at the desk when we go out like at a hotel."

"Thank you, Mae," Callie said. "I guess I'd better put my things away and make a list of what I'm going to need from the mercantile."

"Oh, yes, ma'am," Mae said and opened the door. The jovial high-pitched laughter of young women came drifting in and Mae rolled her eyes. "Tabby must have told another one of her silly jokes. She's your neighbor, by the way, and I'll warn ya now," Mae said, nodding to the wall separating Callie's from the room next door. The redhead grinned and winked. "Tabby enjoys her work and can get right loud when she's at it."

When the girl closed the door, Callie hurried to lock it and tested it with a twist of the knob and a hard tug. Convinced the door was secure, Callie took a minute to study her new abode. The plaster walls had been painted a pale, muted green, but cracks scarred the plaster in places. Callie wrinkled her nose and didn't want to consider what had made the stains running down the wall beside the dulled, brass headboard.

I suppose I could paint to freshen things up. No, I refuse to consider this place my permanent residence.

The single window had no curtain and when

Callie pushed aside the drawn canvas shade, she noted prints on the outside of the glass that looked as though a face had been pressed against it, trying to get a look inside.

Perhaps the former resident liked to put on shows for prospective clients.

Callie lifted her bags onto the bed and took out her clothes.

No sense letting them wrinkle. I have no iron or any way to heat one.

She shook each garment out before hanging it on one of the wooden hangers in the narrow wardrobe. When she'd finished, she studied the meager wardrobe of six skirts, six blouses, and jackets she'd made of coordinating fabrics she could mix and match to expand her ensembles from six to several dozen.

At the washbasin, Callie arranged her comb and brush along with a few pins and ribbons for her hair. She took her bonnets from a bag and set them on the shelf in the wardrobe along with the few sewing things she'd stuffed in at the last minute.

How do you go about stuffing ten years of marriage into three little bags? I had to leave so much behind.

Callie dropped onto the thin, bare mattress again and tears washed down her face.

What did I do to deserve this? Get old? Become barren when I gave birth to my baby and then lose her to a fever? How is that all my fault? I took vows that said for better or for worse until death do us part. I thought Evan did as well.

When the tears had run their course, Callie wiped her eyes, took the filthy chamber pot along with the pitcher from her room, and went out the back door to find the water pump. As she walked down the hall, Callie heard the noises of girls entertaining clients in their rooms. Raucous laughter, grunts, groans, and the pounding of headboards filtered out into the hall.

Callie hurried along with the pitcher of cold water sloshing in her arms and the freshly cleaned pot. Her breath caught in her throat as she pushed the door to her room open and found Matthew Caine standing at her wardrobe, fingering the lace of a dressing gown she'd hung on a hook in the wardrobe.

"What are you doing in my room?" Callie gasped as she stepped to the washstand to set the pitcher into the bowl.

"Well," the tall man said with a grin as he put the frill of lace to his nose, "this is actually one of my rooms and I thought the two of us should have a little talk about the house rules and such." Caine smiled and Callie noticed the long, puckered scar on his right cheek draw up his mouth as he leered down at her.

"House rules?" Callie asked uneasily.

This should be interesting.

Caine moved around the bed and reached Callie's side in two quick strides of his long legs. "Let me have a look at you," he said and pulled the combs from Callie's hair. Her thick chestnut waves cascaded down past her shoulders. Caine fluffed them a bit as she stood stiff with shock and surprise. He stepped back to leer down at Callie, a good foot shorter than Caine's six-feet six-inch height with his boots on.

I've never been treated so rudely. What does he think gives him the right to come into my room uninvited?

"I'd appreciate you taking your hands off me and leaving my room," Callie demanded and tried to jerk her hand from his grasp.

The giant of a man grinned and continued to hold her arm. "That's just what I thought when I first saw you come in. You could still be a money-maker here, even though you have a few years on you." He let his hand slide down over her blouse to caress one of Callie's bosoms. She cringed at his touch and tried to step away.

"You have no right," Callie gasped and drew back her hand to deliver a slap.

"Now, now," Caine said with a chuckle as he grabbed Callie's other slender wrist. "If you're gonna be one of my girls, you're going to need to learn some manners." He dropped one of her arms and twisted the other arm painfully behind Callie's back.

"Evan says you're an average fuck," Caine said, leering into Callie's tear-filled eyes, "but I bet I can train you up to be much better than average." He began fumbling with the buttons on her white cotton blouse. "Now, let's see what we have to work with here." He pulled open the garment and tugged at the ribbon to untie her camisole. The tiny buttons flustered his big fingers and he yanked the camisole open to expose Callie's heavy bosoms. "Yah, those are nice," he said as he caressed one of her nipples with the tip of his finger, causing it to stiffen.

How am I going to get myself out of this mess?

"Let go of me, you beast," Callie screamed and clawed at Caine's big hand. She let out a bloodcurdling scream, but the big man simply grinned down at her.

"That ain't gonna do nothin' for ya, sweetheart," he said with a chuckle and pinched her nipple harder as Callie struggled in his grasp.

"What the hell do you think you're doing, Matthew Caine?" Mae yelled as she came flying through the door with another of the girls from the lobby.

Caine released Callie to glare at Mae. "What I'm

doing is none of your damned business, Ruby, so get the hell out and let me finish with her." He glared down at Callie who fumbled to get her blouse re-buttoned.

"You're more than finished, big man," the other girl said and tugged on Caine's sleeve until he followed her out of Callie's room.

Mae closed the brown six-panel door and turned the key in the lock. "I told you Caine was an ass," Mae snapped. "Why did you let him in your room?"

"I didn't," Callie protested and pushed her hair out of her face. "I went out for water and he was in my room when I got back."

Mae rolled her big green eyes. "That's why I told you to lock your room and take your key with you when you went out," she said. "If you don't, the big ass will go through your things and wait to pounce on you when you get back. He thinks he owns us all and can have a poke whenever the mood strikes."

"Oh, my lord," Callie said and heaved a sigh. "How can you all put up with that?" Callie slipped into her jacket and pulled down her sleeves, rubbing her arm where Caine had twisted it. "If you and your friend hadn't come in, I think he would have …" Callie's eyes filled with tears again as she glanced at the bed.

"Yes," Mae confirmed, "I'm sure that's exactly what he intended. "Don't worry none on that account, though," she said with a grin, "I'm sure Trudy is setting him straight right about now."

"Trudy?"

"The blonde girl who was with me," she said. "When we came in and saw Caine wasn't lazin' in his chair at the counter, I had a feelin' he might be in here harassing you," Mae continued as she stood at Callie's washstand examining one of her pewter hairpins. "I dragged Trudy along because she fancies Caine her intended and wouldn't put up with any bullshit from him."

"Oh, my word," Callie sighed, picturing the slim, blue-eyed young woman who'd tugged Caine from the room.

"I was comin' in to see if you wanted to go with me back up to the mercantile," Mae said as she ran her fingers over the stiff bristles of Callie's hairbrush. "Martin has a new order of fabric in that would be perfect for bed linens and curtains for your room, if you're staying here, that is."

Callie eyed the empty mattress and sighed, "I don't know if I'm staying, but I guess I'm gonna have to do something if I want to have something to sleep on tonight."

CHAPTER 2
THE RAMROD

"Get those cows in pins and settled for the night," Clayton Swift bellowed to his hands. "We'll hold 'em here for the night and see the buyer in the mornin'."

"Where ya headed, boss?" Tom Draper asked as he rode up beside Clayton.

"I need a bath and a hot meal *not* cooked by that worthless excuse of a grubber, Forsythe."

Draper rolled his eyes and wiped his brow with his sleeve. "Ain't that the truth. Where'd ya find him anyhow?"

Clayton shrugged his tired shoulders. "Double-T hired him on for the drive before we left. I got no idea where Thompson found him."

"Sure, weren't at no fine eatery lest they was cookin' fer hogs," Draper said with a chuckle. "I'll see the herd bedded down, boss, and accompany the men into town to keep 'em from tearin' the place up too bad."

"Remind 'em there'll be no pay 'til tomorrow," Clayton warned, "If they get drunk and break up the saloon without the coin to pay for the damages, they'll be spendin' the night in the Ellsworth jail."

Draper grinned and tipped his dusty hat. "Will do, boss. Enjoy your bath and supper."

Clayton turned his horse away from the holding pens at the railhead and headed into town. Ellsworth, Kansas, had taken Abilene's place as the railhead for cattle headed back east two years ago, after the Progressives in Abilene's City Council had banned the sale of alcohol and put restrictions on the whores.

Cowboys don't want to spend months on the hot, dusty trail with nothing to look forward to at the end. If they can't get drunk and dip their weasel in a whore at the end, they don't want to sign on for a drive. When ranchers began having trouble manning crews and the buyers no longer had herds to buy in Abilene, the frustrated cattlemen went to the railroad and insisted a spur be built to Ellsworth where the City Council was much more accommodating to the cowboys and appreciated the business they brought into their town.

Clayton found the mercantile first, where he intended to purchase a new shirt and trousers.

"Excuse me, ladies," Clayton said to two women in the store, "which one of these do you think suits me more?" He held up a bright red calico shirt and another in a dark blue plaid.

The younger of the women put a finger beneath her nose and giggled, but the other, a bit older and possibly the mother of the other, smiled warmly and pointed to the blue one. "That one goes better with your eyes," she said kindly, "and I think that red one might start a stampede."

Clayton hastily refolded the red shirt and returned it to the table. "You're probably right, ma'am," he said with a grin and a wink before taking the garments to the counter and paying for them.

He tucked the fresh shirt trousers under his arm and got a whiff of what the younger woman must have. He left the store for the barber shop, where he hoped to get a much-needed bath, shave, and a haircut. Three months on the trail, sleeping on the ground and living in the same set of clothes, made the stop at the barber Clayton's first at the end of every drive. He usually had an extra set of clothes in his saddlebags, but a rainstorm and a roll in the mud had necessitated a change along the trail.

"How are you, Mr. Swift?" the barber greeted him as he entered the tidy shop. "Which drive are you up with today?"

"The Double-T down by El Paso," Clayton said as he took a seat in the barber's chair.

"You wantin' your regular, Mr. Swift? The barber asked.

"If you please."

"Just sit tight then, while I put the water on the fire for your bath."

Clayton nodded and settled into the chair while he waited. He closed his eyes and the pretty face of the woman in the store came back to him. He'd stood on the boardwalk and waited for a bit until the woman and her daughter had left the mercantile loaded down with packages wrapped in brown paper and tied with string.

The sight of them walking together and laughing, reminded Clayton of the things he'd missed out on, choosing the life of a cowboy. He'd never married—never gotten to know a woman long enough to want to stay in one place. At fifty, he knew he was past the age of thinking about having children. Of course, a man generally needed a wife before begetting children and Clayton didn't have one of those.

"Water should be ready by the time I get done

with your trim," the barber said as he threw a towel around Clayton's neck and shoulders.

They chit-chatted about the weather, the trail, and how Ellsworth was growing.

"We have new folks moving in all the time," the barber said as he scraped stubble from Clayton's cheeks and chin with a sharp straight-razor.

"Of course, the wife and her nagging friends at the church aren't very happy about all the whores in town from Abilene," he said as he wiped the razor clean. "If it was up to them, they'd burn down the damned Ellsworth House with all the tenants locked up inside." He said with a chuckle. "It surely don't hurt me none to see all them pretty faces and perky bosoms sashaying around town, though."

The barber finished with him, and Clayton went into the back room to soak off some of the dirt and some of the aches in the copper tub of hot water.

Maybe I'm getting too old for these three-month drives. Maybe I should find myself a little farm, a warm woman, and leave the cowboyin' to younger men like Draper.

Clayton sat in the water until it cooled, got out and toweled off with a cotton sheet, and dressed in his long-johns, new trousers, and shirt.

"How much do I owe you today?" Clayton asked the busy barber.

The man frowned. "It'll be two bits today, Mr. Swift. With all the new business in town, I thought I should raise my prices a little."

Clayton nodded, dug into his pocket for the coins, and paid the man.

A little is one thing, but two bits for a clip and a bath is double from the last time.

He walked out into the cooler evening air, ran a hand through his clean, damp graying hair, and smiled.

I suppose being clean for the first time in three months is worth two bits.

Clayton turned on the boardwalk and headed toward the Flat Iron. The food there had been good and priced reasonably the last time he'd visited the town.

He went inside the busy cafe and smiled when he saw the pretty woman from the store earlier, sitting alone.

"Well," he said as he walked up to her table, "what do you think?" He pulled at his new shirt. "Are you alone? May I join you?"

She smiled warmly and motion to an empty chair. "The shirt looks and smells very much nicer than your other one."

Clayton took the seat with a smile, "I'm sure of that," he said and offered his hand. "I'm Clay ... Clayton Swift."

"Nice to meet you, Clay," she said with a warm smile and took his hand, "I'm Callie Jamison."

"So, what's good here, Callie Jamison?" he asked as he gazed around the small room.

A couple came into the café and Callie nodded. "I don't recognize you from town, Mr. Swift. Are you new to Ellsworth?"

"I'm up with cattle from Texas," he said and nodded in the direction of the railhead.

"What can I get for you today, Mrs. Jamison," asked a portly man wearing a white apron and his sleeves rolled up above his elbows.

"What does your wife have on the stove today, Mr. Jenkins?" Callie asked.

"She has a nice pigeon pie and we have some fresh elk steaks too," Jenkins said.

"Steak surely sounds good to a hungry cowboy," Clayton said. "What's that come with?"

"Pan-fried potatoes and beans," Mr. Jenkins said with a glance at Callie.

"I'll have a plate of that pigeon pie," Callie said, "and a cup of cider, if you have it."

"Yes, indeed, ma'am," Mr. Jenkins said. "And you sir, what would you like to drink?"

"Coffee, if you please, sir," Clayton said.

Mr. Jenkins nodded and walked away toward the entrance to the kitchen.

"Where's your daughter tonight?" Clayton asked.

"My daughter?" Callie asked with her face screwed up in confusion.

"They youngster you were in the store with today. I took her to be your daughter," Clayton said, "She wasn't?"

Callie grinned at the cowboy. "No, Mae is just a girl who lives in the same boarding house. I was out picking up a few supplies and Mae came along with me to the mercantile."

"I beg your pardon, then," Clayton said and doffed his hat. "The girl had a look about her. She resembles ya some."

"Well, thank you," Callie said with her cheeks turning pink, "Mae's a pretty girl."

"So, you live over at the boarding house?" Clayton asked with a raised brow.

"Well, hello there, teacher lady," someone said, and Callie looked up to see Marvin Taylor, the town drunk, staring at her, and drooling down his stubbled chin. "Didn't I see ya today out back the Ellsworth gettin' water from the pump?" the man mumbled drunkenly and stepped over to drape an arm over Callie's shoulders. "You decide to change professions over the summer months?" he asked, staring down at Callie's bosoms.

"Excuse me?" Callie yelped and shrugged Marvin off.

"Hey, now," Marvin snapped.

"Mister," Clayton said and stood, "I don't think the lady is interested in your attention. Why don't you mosey on out of here and leave the lady be?"

The drunken man snorted, "She sure ain't no lady if she's livin' at the Ellsworth," Marvin sneered, scowling down at Callie. "There's only one kinda woman lives at the Ellsworth and they sure ain't no ladies."

Mr. Jenkins came over to see what the commotion was and carried their drinks with him. "Is Marvin making a nuisance of himself?" he asked as he set the drinks on the table and took the drunk in hand. "I've told you before, Marvin, you can only come to the back door for your supper." Mr. Jenkins led Marvin back to the kitchen and soon returned with their plates of steaming food.

"This looks good," Clayton said as he cut into the succulent steak. He popped a piece into his mouth and closed his eyes as he chewed. "I haven't tasted food like this in a month of Sundays," he said with a contented look on his handsome, cleanly shaven face except for a very full white mustache framing his mouth.

Callie picked at her plate of pigeon pie. The embarrassing encounter with Marvin had spoiled her appetite. She could only imagine what the cowboy must think of her after Marvin's rant about the kind of women who resided at The Ellsworth.

After several bites from his plate, Clayton asked, "So what brought you to be livin' at Ellsworth House?"

"My *former* husband," Callie said and stabbed a bite of pigeon in her pie.

"All right," Clayton said with a raised white brow.

"My husband, Evan, set me aside for the child next door, and dropped me off at the Ellsworth until I can find something more suitable."

"Do you have the means to do that?" Clayton asked.

"Not at the moment," Callie admitted. "I teach at the school during the winter months when the children aren't needed in the fields, but until then, I'm going to have to find some other income source," she said with a slight shrug of her shoulders.

"Not the way the other women at the Ellsworth do, I hope," he said with a nervous grin.

"No," she said, blushing again. "Though, I don't know why not," Callie snorted, "I've spent the past ten years sleeping with a man, who obviously cared little about me, to keep a roof over my head." She shrugged her shoulders. "Is that so much different from what those women do?"

Clayton gave her a thoughtful look across the table. "Well, when I think on it that way, you may have a point."

CHAPTER 3
SHE FALLS EVEN LOWER

C allie watched the cowboy leave the Flat Iron and smiled. It had been a long time since she'd had a pleasant conversation with a man over supper. Over the past year, Evan had become more distant, spending hours away from the ranch until one afternoon while out foraging for berries, Callie had come upon him and Polly Hardin rolling naked in the bushes.

Now the girl claimed she was pregnant, and Evan said he wanted to marry her.

He's fifty-five years old, for heaven's sake. Does he really think he can deal with a screaming infant and a surly teenage girl for a wife?

Lost in her thoughts, Callie didn't see Mr. and Mrs. Martin approach her table until she heard the skinny owner of the mercantile clear his throat.

"Good evening, Mrs. Jamison," Mr. Martin said without a smile on his face.

"Good evening," Callie said cordially.

They both look like they just bit into a sour pickle.

"I must admit that I'm concerned, Mrs. Jamison," Mr. Martin said with a frown. "My wife tells me you were in the store today with one of those little tarts from the Ellsworth. Is that true?"

Callie glanced up at Amelia Martin. The mercantile owner's wife refused to look Callie in the eye. "I'm sure that if your wife said I was in the store, then I was in the store. I believe I spent about eight dollars," Callie added.

"You have read the morals clause in your employment contract, have you not?" Mr. Martin asked glaring down at Callie with his beady brown eyes that reminded Callie of the hawk that pestered her chickens out on the ranch.

"I have," she replied, with an air of concern for the first time. "But I don't understand how shopping with someone can be seen as immoral."

"If you do not, Mrs. Jamison, then I fear we've made a serious mistake in renewing your employment with the school. First, you are out with a soiled woman, acting as though you didn't have a care in the world," he snarled, "and then we come in here tonight to find you consorting with a man in public, who is not your husband."

"I no longer have a husband, sir," Callie snapped.

"No longer have a husband?" Mrs. Martin gasped, wide-eyed. "What on earth …"

"In that case, I'm sorry to say, you no longer qualify to teach the young, impressionable children of Ellsworth, Mrs. Jamison," Mr. Martin said. "Luckily, we have another viable candidate for the position in young Polly Hardin, one of your former charges, I believe."

I can't believe this, first, the little bitch steals my husband, and now she's after my job.

Callie took a deep breath, "Well, I hope you enjoy the wedding." Callie gathered her bag, stood, and pushed past the Martins.

"What wedding?" Mrs. Martin asked.

"Evan and Polly's," she said matter-of-factly in a loud voice so the other diners could hear. "It seems someone has gotten little Polly Hardin with child, and Evan thinks it could be his, so he's set me aside and plans to marry the little tart," Callie poked Mr. Martin in the chest with her finger. "Perhaps you should have given her a copy of that morals clause to read, though reading comprehension was never Polly's long suit. I don't recall her passing the State Teacher's Exam either. When did she take that?"

Callie pushed past the gawking couple and stormed out the door with the other diners beginning to whisper amongst themselves. She was certain Polly's disgrace would be common knowledge all over Ellsworth and she grinned mischievously.

Now, what am I supposed to do? The job at the school only paid three dollars a month, but it paid for my incidentals like fabric for new dresses. Evan must pay my rent, but I still must eat. The Flat Iron isn't free, and I certainly don't intend to pay for my meals the way Mae and the others do.

CHAPTER 4
SHE STILL MUST EAT

Callie stormed into the lobby of the Ellsworth House boiling mad. Four women sat in the lobby with their dressing gowns open over corsets displaying mounded bosoms. Two of them grinned at her as she passed by but didn't offer a greeting. From behind the counter, Caine glared at her. Callie ignored him, relieved she wouldn't find him waiting in her dark room.

She locked the door behind her as soon as she was inside, where the dim glow of the lamp she'd lit before leaving, cast the room in flickering shades of amber. Callie turned up the flame and the empty room brightened.

She smiled at the new lamp, her one indulgence of the day. For the most part, Callie had purchased only the essentials at the mercantile; linen for a mattress covering, a feather pillow, some soap for bathing, fabric for a coverlet and curtains, and thread.

The lamp, with its lavender frosted glass globe and oil reservoir on a dulled brass base, had been pure fancy and Callie had come close to returning it to the shelf several times. Fifty cents for a pretty piece of glass was frivolous, she told herself, but Mae had pointed out how the glass matched the violets in the fabric she'd chosen for her coverlet, pillow slips, and curtains.

Callie ran her hand over the smooth glass globe.

After the day I've had, I'm entitled to a bit of frivolity even if it did cost half a day's rent in this house of ill-repute.

The wrapped parcels remained on the mattress where she'd left them before leaving for her dinner. Callie unwrapped the heavy parcel of folded fabric. Sewing had always been one of her joys and she intended to make this horrible room beautiful. She moved the other small packages and spread a sheet of linen over the ugly, stained ticking. Mrs. Martin had cut the two-yard pieces from the bolt, so all Callie would need to do was hem the cut ends.

I'll tend to that tomorrow.

She tucked one piece around the mattress to secure it and spread the other to use as a cover. The unwrapped pillows, Callie tossed to the top of the bed. Pillow slips and a quilted coverlet would be a project for the days to come.

Satisfied she had a somewhat comfortable bed for the night, Callie slipped out of her severe black suit, tossed aside the camisole Cane had ripped and wriggled into her plain, cotton nightdress. She ran her hand over the soft, worn fabric and grinned at her reflection.

I doubt I'd attract many clients, sitting out in the lobby, wearing this old thing.

As Callie was about to crawl into bed, a woman's screaming curses came from down the hall, and she threw on her dressing gown before going to the door and peeking out.

A half-dressed cowboy stumbled toward the rear door as Trudy tossed his boots at him and called him names Callie had never heard come from a woman's mouth before.

I suspect I'm going to acquire a whole colorful new vocabulary while living here.

Mae saw Callie, trudged up the hall with a grin on her face, and said, "Just another night with a drive here in town."

"Oh, my," Callie said and stepped out into the hall. She pulled her dressing gown tight around her and secured it with the cotton sash.

"That's pretty," Mae said, pointing to Callie's lace-trimmed dressing gown. "Where'd you get it? I've never seen one like it at Martin's."

"I made it," Callie said, brushing aside the compliment with red cheeks.

The rear door slammed as the cowboy departed Ellsworth House and Mae motioned for Callie to follow as she trotted down the hall to Trudy's door. Several of the women huddled around the disheveled, little blonde.

"What happened?" Mae asked as she pushed her way closer to the weeping young woman.

"Look what that grabby son-of-a-bitch did to my new duds," she exclaimed, holding a strip of lace torn from the top of her silk camisole. "I just got this in yesterday from St. Louis," she sobbed, "and look what he did. I paid five dollars for it and the bloomers that match and now it's ruined."

Many of the women nodded in commiseration and Mae put an arm around her friend. "Come on, sweetie," Mae cooed softly as she ushered the weeping girl back into her room. "Let's get you out of this and into your nightdress." She gently undid the tiny pearl buttons remaining on the flimsy garment, slid it off Trudy's heaving shoulders and tossed it to the floor with the band of lace trailing behind.

While Mae helped Trudy into her nightdress, Callie bent and picked up the discarded garment, amazed at the light, soft fabric between her fingers. She'd never felt silk before. In the glow of Trudy's lamp, Callie saw two of the tiny buttons torn from the garment and scooped them up. She examined the garment and smiled.

"Don't cry, Trudy," Callie told the weeping girl. "I can fix this for you as good as new."

Trudy jerked her head up, wide-eyed. "You can?"

"Sure," Callie said with a smile. "I just have to regather the lace and tack it back down," she said examining the garment a little closer, "stitch up the buttonholes, and replace these little buttons." Callie displayed one of the tiny buttons she'd found. "I'll have it back to you tomorrow," Callie assured her with a smile.

"Now," Mae said softly as she wiped Trudy's tear-streaked face with a wet cloth, "you see. It's gonna be just fine."

"What in hell's name has you birds all riled up now?" Caine growled from the doorway.

"That fucking cowboy you sent back here," Trudy snapped, glaring at the tall man, "tore my new silk camisole, trying to get at my damned nipples." She shook her head and said to Mae and Callie, "I can't fathom why they need to see my nipples for a simple poke. Why can't they just be happy with what's between my legs?"

"Well," Caine snarled, "get yourself together and get back to the lobby. The night is young, and we have two damned drives in town." Caine noticed Callie for the first time and grinned. "You should join them. I could have you broken into the business in no time at all. Some of those young cowboys might fancy poking a mother-type like you."

"Oh, shut up," Trudy told him with a scowl as she marched past the unnaturally tall man into the hall. "Callie's gonna fix my camisole, so you just leave her alone, Matthew Caine."

Caine simply rolled his dark eyes, stepped back into the hallway, and followed the little blonde.

"That man is a real pig," Mae growled beside Callie.

"Aren't they all?" Callie said, thinking of her former husband.

At Callie's door, Mae asked, "Can you really fix that?" She nodded to the camisole clutched in Callie's hand. "These are our work clothes, you know," she said, running a delicate, freckled hand over her simple cotton dressing gown, "we spend most of our money on them and try to get as much wear out of them as we can."

"Sure," she said, taking what Mae said into consideration. "I'll get to it first thing in the morning when I have more light. Do you think I could get a chair?"

Mae shrugged. "There might be one or two down in the basement. I'll ask the asshole," she said and nodded toward the lobby counter.

"I'd appreciate that," Callie said and went into her room where she locked her door before she draped the camisole on her vanity then crawled beneath her sheet.

A rooster's crowing woke Callie as the sun rose. She rolled on the thin mattress and listened to the quiet. The night had been anything but. Raucous laughter from the women in the lobby and the tromping of boots down the hall had kept Callie awake into the wee hours of the morning.

Is this what my life is to be now? How much lower can I possibly fall?

Callie rousted herself from bed to squat over the chamber pot she'd cleaned thoroughly the day before. No sounds other than the occasional creaking of the walls as the building settled could be heard.

I suppose everyone sleeps in when they are up all night working.

She was happy for the hardy supper the night before. She wouldn't be going across the street for breakfast. While she lay awake the night before, her financial situation had plagued her, and Callie had come to the conclusion that one meal a day would have to be her limit until she could find an income source.

I could certainly use a cup of coffee, though.

CHAPTER 5
TEXAS LIL

As Callie took a seat to begin sewing, a soft knock sounded at her door. She rose, hurried across the room, and cracked the door. A stout, handsome woman dressed in black stood in the hall, leaning on a silver-handled cane.

"I heard another old bird had moved into The House," the woman said with a broad smile on her powdered face. "I'm Lil. May I come in?"

Callie opened the door and held it for Lil as she sashayed regally through, peering around the shabby room.

"Ruthie never did much with this room," Lil sighed. "She was classless trash if I ever saw it."

"How long have you been living here?" Callie asked and motioned toward the padded bench in front of the vanity.

"In Kansas, in Ellsworth, or in this dump?" Lil asked as she sat.

"All the above?" Callie said with an uneasy grin.

The older woman ran her wrinkled hand over wavy, silver hair that looked fine and soft. "Well, let me see," she sighed heavily. "I left Texas several years ago and landed in Abilene. They called me Texas Lil back then," she added proudly. "I shepherded some girls in a house there until we got run out of town by the damned Progressives and their prohibitionist policies," Lil said with a snarl. "I followed some of the girls here two years ago and thought I might retire in style and buy a little house with a yard and everything," she sighed, "but it didn't work out and I landed here in this lovely abode." She took a deep breath. "So, what's your story, sugar? How'd you end up in this sorry excuse for a crib? You're not in the trade, are you?"

"Lord, no," Callie gasped. " I just turned forty. Who'd want to pay for an old woman like me?"

"You'd be surprised, sugar," Lil said and winked. "You'd be surprised."

Callie studied the woman intently. Her dress was well-made from good quality linen and probably expensive. She wore a carnelian cameo brooch at her throat set in gold and gold earbobs dangled from her creased earlobes. Gemstone rings decorated most of her fingers.

I bet she was a good-looking woman in her day. I'd never have taken her for a former whore. She looks more like a church matron, except for the jewelry and the rouge on her cheeks.

"I had a husband," Callie began with a sigh. "He decided he wanted a younger woman, divorced me, and dumped me here," she said and motioned around the shabby room.

"Divorce," Lil spat. "In my day, if a man got an itch for strange cunny, he just found a whore for the night and kept his family intact. Now he divorces his wife," she snarled, shaking her head. "It's disgraceful, tearing apart a family, and hurting the children."

"Do you have children, Lil?" Callie asked casually and picked up Trudy's torn camisole.

"I have a son ... somewhere," she sighed and

shrugged her broad shoulders. "We're what you'd call … estranged. How 'bout you, sugar?"

Callie shook her head and studied her stitches. "I had a little girl," she whispered, "but she went back to God two years after he gave her to me. I couldn't have any others after her."

"I'm sorry to hear that, sugar," Lil said and studied Callie as she replaced the tiny buttons on the piece of silk fabric.

"You thinking about taking up the trade? Silk frillies like that are expensive," Lil said with a raised brow.

"No!" Callie exclaimed and looked up from the dainty camisole. "This belongs to a girl down the hall," she said with an embarrassed grin. "Some cowboy got a little out of hand last night and tore it."

Lil grinned. "They tend to do that after a few months on the trail."

"Where is your boy now?" Callie asked.

"He's far from a boy now," Lil said with a slight frown. "I haven't seen him in close to forty years."

"That's a long time," Callie said as she worked on regathering the lace to attach to the camisole.

"He left home when he was fifteen," Lil sighed. "He couldn't take the humiliation of having the town whore for a mother."

"Were you … when …" Callie couldn't bring herself to spit out the question and blushed.

"Was I a whore when I had my son?" Lil finished the sentence and grinned. "All these girls here have a sad story to tell as to how they got into this life," Lil said, "and I'm no different."

"Like you," she continued, "I had a husband down in Texas, but he up and got himself killed by Indians. I was alone and my family was all back in Georgia. I couldn't travel home with a new baby to take care of, so I started taking a few clients in the privacy of my house from the nearby settlement. Texas was a wild place back then."

She stood and began pacing the room. "When my boy got bigger and began to sort things out, I moved us into town and worked out of a hotel." Lil pursed her lips and sighed.

"But your son was getting older and boys at school exchange stories," Callie said, remembering the overheard conversations between some of her students at the school.

"I'm afraid so," Lil sighed, "and he rode away one day to join a cattle drive and … and just never came back." She raised her hands and exhaled.

"Aside from losing my boy over it," the woman said, "the business was good to me. If you should decide to dip your toe in the water, do it," Lil said as she moved toward the door, her heavy skirt swishing over her petticoat as she walked. She turned with a serious look on her face and pointed her finger at Callie.

"But don't you ever look back with regret on your decision, sugar. A woman alone has very few options. We must make our own opportunities in this life, Callie, because no man is going to hand one to us. Men only take," Lil said as she opened the door, "they never give."

Callie considered Lil's words as she finished stitching Trudy's camisole. She held the flimsy garment up when she finished and studied it closely.

I've never owned anything like this in my life. I got married in a homemade dress and I've made my own clothes all my married life. Would it be so bad to sell my favors to a man? I gave my favors to Evan for ten years and look at what he did to me. These women have no emotional ties to the men they bed, and they earn a good wage for their time. What's the real harm?

Callie delivered the repaired garment to Trudy as the girl sat in the lobby. The petite young woman studied the garment, tugged gently at the lace, and buttoned and rebuttoned it, testing the buttons and slits.

Trudy jumped to her feet and wrapped her arms around Callie's neck, while some of the other girls studied the repaired camisole.

"Thank you so much, Callie," she gushed. "It looks just like it did when I took it out of the box." Trudy wiped her eyes. "What do I owe you for fixing it?"

"Not a thing," Callie said with a shake of her head.

"The old lady at the laundry would have charged at least fifteen cents," Mae said, "and wouldn't have done nearly as nice a job. I have a few things that need mending and I'd be glad to pay," Mae said with a grin.

"Me too," some of the other girls added.

"What would you charge to make me one of those pretty dressing gowns too?" Mae asked with a raised brow.

"You going to buy the fabric or me?" Callie asked with a sly smile.

Maybe I can make a little dinner coin without calling that morality clause into question after all.

CHAPTER 6
THE LONG RIDE

Clayton rode south toward Texas with the Double-T Ranch's bank draft for the herd he'd driven to Ellsworth in his pocket. If he pressed hard, he'd be there in three weeks and be ready to take out another herd the following week. It would be the final drive of the season.

He closed his tired eyes in the saddle and saw Callie's crystal-blue ones. No woman had affected Clayton the way this one had—not ever.

I just met her, and I can't get her out of my damned mind. She certainly doesn't seem like any whore I've ever met. She's clean and wholesome. I bet she wouldn't let her kid grow up in the same house with her if she was really a whore. Didn't that drunk call her the town schoolteacher? She looks like a schoolteacher.

Clayton sat at his campfire, chewing on a strip of jerky. It had been a long day and he needed sleep. He rummaged in his saddlebag for a piece of paper and pencil. Maybe he'd write her a letter.

Dear Callie,

I'm writing this by the light of my cam fire, so please forgive the dirt on the paper and the poor penmanship. I can't hon-

estly say why I'm writing this letter, but I felt I had to. I'm on my way to El Paso and will probably be back in Ellsworth sometime in September. I hope you will find it in your heart to agree to see me while I am there. I will post this in the next town, and I hope it gets to you before then.

Please know you have been on my mind since I got your opinion on the shirt. I will write again and hope you get the letter in a timely fashion.

Yours,

Clayton Swift

Clayton folded the paper into an envelope so it could be posted. Hopefully, the postmaster in the next town would have something to seal it with. He slid the letter back into his saddlebag before crawling into his blankets.

Coyotes yipped in the distance and Clayton banked his fire before pulling the blanket up to his chin. He ran a hand over his long graying hair and sighed.

Sleeping on the hard, cold ground with coyotes skulking around is something for younger men. Maybe I've found that warm woman I could settle down with. Maybe I'll take her back to Fredericksburg and settle down. Well, maybe not Fredericksburg.

Coyotes yipped throughout the night and Clayton slept fitfully on the cold sandy soil of the Indian Nations. He rose with the sun and boiled some coffee over the last embers of the night's fire.

Clayton cleared his camp and saddled his mare. The horse was getting old, but who wasn't. He ran his hand over his face, his cheeks stubbled with gray whiskers.

"You ready to go again, Dolly?" The horse whinnied and Clayton patted her neck. "I know, I'm tired too."

He saddled the horse and secured his gear. The trail south through the Nations was relatively safe and Clayton stopped at the first settlement he came to and posted his letter to Callie Jamison in Ellsworth, Kansas. The postmaster had assured Clayton delivery would be made timely. The town was on the regular Butterfield route and the stage picked up their mail pouches on a weekly basis.

Clayton had been skeptical, gazing around at the scattered houses and slipshod constructed buildings along the rutted, dirt path they called a street. He said a prayer as he left the town for the letter's arrival in Ellsworth before his return in September.

The early June sun blazed on the western horizon when he and Dolly crested a rise and Clayton saw a green meadow with a wide creek running through. The brush along the creek would supply wood for a fire and cover should he and Dolly need it.

"That looks like a fine place to camp tonight, Dolly," he said as he urged the horse forward. "There's green grass for you and maybe a nice fat fish in that creek for me."

The valley appeared devoid of human habitation and Clayton liked that. He didn't want to trespass on any settler's homestead and he certainly didn't want a run-in with any of the tribes.

Clayton made his camp in a clearing beside the creek and threw a line into the water baited with a bit of jerky. He was rewarded with a sturdy ten-inch catfish. The slick fish had nearly slipped back into the water as he tried to get the hook out of his gullet, but Clayton had managed to trap it before it flopped back into the muddy creek.

The fish sizzled in a small cast-iron pan Clayton carried in his gear when a rider approached his camp.

Damnit, I just wanted to eat a meal in peace.

"Hey, neighbor," a grizzled, old man called from his mule, "mind if an old man and his ride share your camp for the night?"

"I suppose not," Clayton said cordially.

"Thank ya kindly," the old man said and slid off the swaybacked mule. "Mind if I stake Bessie here out with your horse? She's like me and has a hankerin' for a bit of company at night."

"Go ahead," Clayton mumbled as he used his knife to flip the fish in the pan.

After staking out his mule in the tall grass, the old man trudged through the knee-high grass to join Clayton by the fire. He lugged his saddle and gear over and dropped it beside Clayton's.

"Got these some ways back on the trail," he said and held up two fat quail by their legs. "Mind if I cook 'em up on your fire?"

"Be my guest," Clayton said as he took his skillet off the fire.

"I'll just go down to the creek and skin 'em up. Name's Hawkins, by the way. Most folks just call me Hawk," the old man said as he walked toward the creek with an uneven gait, carrying the birds and a canvas bag Clayton suspected held his cooking utensils.

Clayton inspected the fish with his knife, decided it needed a few more minutes, and returned the skillet to the fire. He pulled it off again when Hawk came lumbering back with his two skinned and cleaned birds.

"Mind if'n I use your skillet?" the old man asked as he rummaged in the canvas bag. He pulled out a blue, enameled tin plate and handed it to Clayton.

"Here's some cress I pulled by that creek there," Hank said and handed Clayton a hand full of bright green leaves. "It's mighty good eats with fish."

Clayton took the greens and the old man arranged the birds in the skillet after scooping some lard from a tin into it. "Wouldn't be able ta get by without my pig-fat," he said with a chuckle. "Where ya hail from?" the old man asked as he watched over his birds sizzling in the pan.

"I'm on my way to El Paso from Ellsworth," Clayton said.

"On your way back from one o' them cattle drives?"

"Yep, and my name's Clayton," he said and popped a bite of flaky white fish into his mouth followed by some of the peppery-tasting greens. "How 'bout you?"

"It's a pleasure ta make your acquaintance," the old man said as he turned his birds in the pan. "I'm from all over," he sighed. "I was borned in Illinois, or so my mama told me, but I growed up in Missouri. My daddy was a gambler. He rode the riverboats and Mama tended the farm and us youngins."

"Must have been a tough woman," Clayton said and took another bite.

"That's a fact," Hank sighed. "She kept us fed when Daddy didn't come home with money and tilled the ground when he wasn't home to do it." He stared off across the field and scratched his balding gray head. "She fought injuns too. The woman was a damned fine shot ... and with one of them old cap 'n ball muskets ta boot."

"Impressive," Clayton said with a smile. "I'm gonna go get some water," he said with the empty coffee pot in his hand.

"That sounds right nice," Hawk called after him. "I've got some fresh grounds here in my sack."

He seems harmless enough and willing to share his supplies with a stranger. That says a lot.

Clayton returned to the fire, scooped some of Hawks fresh ground coffee into the pot, and set it over the fire to boil. Soon the aroma of freshly brewed coffee joined that of the frying birds.

"So, where was you reared?" Hawk asked as he turned his birds again. "You got the sound of a Texan 'bout ya."

"Yep," Clayton replied. "I was born and grew up around Fredericksburg."

The old man's face lit up with a smile. "I know Fredericksburg," he said. "Spent some time there in my wayward youth." He winked and took the skillet off the fire. "Knew a woman there once," he said with an impish grin on his grizzled face.

"Is that a fact?" Clayton said uneasily as he poured two cups of coffee.

"Her name was Lil," Hawk said as he took the cup Clayton offered. "Probably the most amazing woman I ever knowed 'side from Mama."

"How so?" Clayton asked before gulping down the hot coffee.

"Knew her no 'count husband too," Hawk said as he tore a leg from one of the birds and began gnawing the meat off it. "He were a gambler too," the old man said as he chewed, "but he weren't no good at it. When he got hisself shot by injuns he left Lil with men comin' after 'er for his debts." Hawk shook his head. "Even after what she done for the damned town they come after her."

"What did she do for the town?" Clayton asked with a raised silver brow.

Hawk pulled another chunk of meat from the bird and put it to his mouth. "Back then," he said, "the injuns was still runnin' wild an' raidin' settlements. Fredericksburg weren't even really Fredericksburg yet, just a bunch of German farmers and a tradin' post." He stuffed the meat into his mouth and chewed.

After washing it down with coffee, Hawk continued. "One day ol' Red Horse an' his bunch attacked."

"What's that got to do with this woman?" Clayton pressed.

"I'm getting' to it," the old man scolded. "Well, Lil was home with her baby and her man was there, but sleepin' off another drunk," he said, shaking his head. "I never knowed what such a pretty woman saw in that drunken fool."

Hawk emptied his cup and poured another. "Those Comanches were settin' fire ta farms all 'cross the Republic," Hawk hissed.

"And what did this heroic Lil do?" Clayton asked again.

"Saved the damned settlement is what she done," Hawk said, staring wide-eyed across the fire. "When they come ta 'er place, Lil went outside an' offered 'erself up ta Red Horse and 'is boys ifn they'd move on ta the next settlement an' leave Fredericksburg alone."

"And that worked?" Clayton asked incredulously. "The raiding party left the town alone just because a woman let them all give her a poke?"

"Ifn you'd ever seen Lil, you'd understand, boy," Hawk sighed. "She was a beauty." Hawk closed his eyes, pulling at memories. "I can just imagine what them injuns thought when Lil walked out of that cabin buck-naked and made that offer to 'em."

Clayton swallowed hard and threw the fish carcass into the fire. "And her husband? Where was he during all this?"

"Cowerin' inside with the baby," Hawk grunted. "His were the only life lost that night."

"Fighting for his wife's honor and protecting his child?" Clay asked nervously.

"Hell no," Hawk replied. "After Red Horse had 'is turn with Lil, he went in the house and cut the fool's throat for allowing 'is woman ta fight 'is battles while he hid inside." He grinned across the fire. "Them Comanches don't take kindly to cowardice in a man be he injun or white."

"And letting the band of raiders have a poke saved the settlement? They just rode away?" Clayton growled.

"Rode away just like that," Hawk said and swung his arm through the smoke from the dwindling fire, "and they never come back to harass Fredericksburg again neither," Hawk spit into the fire. "Fat lot of good it done Lil, though."

"What do you mean? Wasn't she lauded as a heroine for her brave sacrifice?"

"Hardly," Hawk spat, "They treated 'er like soiled goods. The women crossed the street so they wouldn't have to bump into 'er … and the men … well the men treated 'er like a whore." Hawk took a swallow of his coffee. "She were a pretty widow woman with a baby. In most settlements, she'd have suitors lining up at 'er door."

"But not there?"

"Oh," Hawk grunted, "they lined up at 'er door all right, but it weren't with no offers of marriage and respectability. No," he spat, "They all just wanted their chance at a poke. They said that if she'd give herself to injun bucks then she should feel lucky of an offer from a good white man." Hawk took a deep breath and shrugged his shoulders. "After a while, with no husband to provide for 'er an' the child, and no assistance from the settlement, Lil started lettin' 'em have a poke," he said and a toothy grin creased his wrinkled face, "but Lil made 'em all pay."

Clayton rubbed his eyes. "Is this woman still in Fredericksburg?"

"No," Hawk said sadly. "When 'er boy up an' run off, it broke Lil's heart and I think she moved to get away from the sad memories," the old man emptied his cup.

"I went back there with the thought on askin' 'er ta marry up with me, but Lil was already gone." The old man took a breath. "I heard once she'd moved up to Kansas; Dodge maybe, lookin' for the boy."

"It's understandable why he'd leave," Clayton said. "What boy would want to live in the same house as the town whore?"

"She mighta been the damned town whore," Hawk snapped, "but it weren't no doin' o' hern an' she loved that boy," he said, pointing his gnarled old finger at Clayton. "She made sure he had good clothes an' sent 'im ta school even though that ungrateful lot in town didn't want 'im in their school."

Hawk gave a little laugh. "Lil went to them town fathers an' told 'em she'd make a public notice of all her local customers if'n they didn't let the boy go to their damned school." Hawk laughed again. "Most of them town fathers visited Lil once a week," the old man said with a wink.

"It still must have been hard on the boy," Clayton sighed. "It was probably better for the both of them that he left. She could go on with her business without the worry of a child and he could find a life of his own without shame and ridicule."

"I s'pose," Hawk said with a yawn. "I wondered over the years ifn she ever caught up with 'im, though." He stretched his skinny frame and stood. "I hope she did," the old man said softly before hobbling to the bushes to relieve himself.

"She didn't," Clay whispered to himself as he stood to do the same.

CHAPTER 7
REUNION

Callie sat in the chair she and Mae had found in the basement and hauled up the stairs. The September sun felt good on her shoulders as she stitched lace onto a new dressing gown for Mae.

Her good deed, repairing Trudy's camisole, had turned into a thriving business. Not only the women at Ellsworth House came to her with garments in need of repair, but also other women practicing the trade in the town. Respectable women in Ellsworth wouldn't use seamstresses who did business with the working girls, which left a void Callie had been more than happy to fill.

She looked up when someone knocked on her door. "Come on in," she called, "it's unlocked."

Mae pushed open the door and came in, holding an envelope in her hand.

"You got another letter," she said with a grin, waving the folded and sealed piece of paper. "I bet it's another one from that smitten cowboy." Mae's smile brightened the room as much as the September sun.

Callie smiled with anticipation. This would be the third letter from him since he'd left in June. She hadn't written him back because he'd told her not to. He never knew where he would be from one week to the next.

She set aside her work and reached for the letter. "Well, give it to me."

"What will you give me if I do?" Mae said, giggling as she taunted Callie with the letter.

"What I won't give you is a good, hard kick in the behind," Callie scolded playfully, "now give it to me."

"Oh, very well," Mae said and handed Callie the letter. "I'll leave you to it, then," she said, smiling, and left the room.

She's nothing more than a silly girl in a woman's body.

Callie recognized the neat script on the letter. She tore away the seal and opened the carefully folded piece of paper. Lines written neatly in pencil filled the page and Callie smiled as she began to read.

Dear Callie,

I write to you again by the light of my campfire. I delivered the bank draft to the Double-T and am now putting together another crew to ride north. It's the same men, for the most part. Draper will ramrod for me and the other fellas will follow along. The only change we are making for this drive is the cook. The last one was a disappointment and a drive runs much smoother with a good cook in the chuck wagon. I anticipate arrival in Ellsworth the third week of September and hope my letters have been arriving. I have been posting them directly with Butterfield. I'm told that is a much more reliable course to take. I hope you will agree to see me again. I also hope you have found more suitable lodgings since my last visit. A re-

spectable woman shouldn't be living in a house of ill-repute.

Again, I think of you every day. I see your eyes when I close mine. You also visit me in my dreams. I look forward to seeing you again in the flesh.

Yours, Clayton Swift

CALLIE READ the letter three times. In all her years, she'd never received letters like his. He dreamed about her? He saw her eyes when he closed his? Some women would call that romantic.

Get hold of yourself, Callie. You're not one of those silly girls you read about in the dime-novels from the apothecary.

The calendar on her wall said today was the fifteenth day of September. She counted down the rows of boxes and saw that this was the third week of the month. Her heart quickened in her chest, but she knew no drive had arrived in town yet. If there had been, the lobby would be full of girls displaying their wares.

I'll ask Mae if she has heard when the next drive is expected. The girls always seem to know days ahead of time.

Someone knocked again. "Come in," Callie called as she hurriedly refolded the letter and slipped it into the pocket of her simple gingham dress.

Lil came through the door carrying a pile of folded garments. Callie rushed to take them from the woman who wobbled a bit without her cane.

"Oh, thank you, sugar," Lil huffed as she dropped onto the edge of the bed. "Those are the dresses I told you about. I'll never know why I've kept them in my trunk all this time. I've toted them all over Texas and now Kansas," she sighed. "I suppose I didn't want to let go of my glory days as the widely sought-after Texas Lil," she said with a flourish of her bejeweled hand. "I'm past all that now, so take them apart and reuse the fabric." She rolled her eyes and smiled. "Lord knows some of those damned skirts have nine yards in them."

"Thank you, Lil," Callie said, brushing her hand over deep blue velvet. "What do I owe you?"

"Oh, please," the older woman said with a dismissive wave, "You don't owe me a thing. They're just old used things that smell like mothballs and cedar."

"Nonsense," Callie scolded and reached into her pocket. She took out a gold dollar she'd received from a woman for making a ruffled dancehall skirt. "Take this," Callie said and handed Lil the coin.

Lil picked up the heavy coin and studied it. "I remember when I made ten of these a day," she said sadly before dropping it into her pocket. "Thank you, sugar. I can use it. I've been living off my savings for the past two years."

"Go have a nice dinner at The Flat Iron," Callie said. I think they have chicken and dumplings today."

"Only if you'll come with me," the older woman said with a smile on her rouged lips. "I hate eating alone." She stood and gazed around the room. "You've really prettied-up this place." She ran a hand over the pillow slips made with fabric covered in violets and sprigs of bright spring greenery. It matched the coverlet on the bed, as well as the curtains.

"Thank you," Callie said, blushing. "It's akin to polishing a pig, though," she sneered, gazing at the cracked, but freshly painted plaster wall, "but I needed to do something to make it look a little homier and," she added wrinkling her nose, "cover those ghastly stains."

"I should have you do something like this for my room," Lil said, "What I have has been traveling with me for years and I'm weary of looking at it."

"I'd be happy to," Callie told the older woman.

"I'm having that ass, Caine, move me down to the second floor," Lil sighed, "I'm too damned old for all those stairs and I'm trying to wean myself away from that damned cane."

"Let me know when," Callie said, "and I'll help you move your things."

The old woman gave a snort. "Most women my age, have a house full of *things*. This old whore has two trunks and every *thing* she owns fits into them and a couple of old carpet bags."

"Oh, my," Callie sighed sympathetically.

"Let's go have some chicken and dumplings, sugar. I'm so hungry I could chew shoe-leather."

They walked through the lobby and Callie noted all the settees were filled with women in their work clothes. She fingered the letter in her pocket and smiled. Maybe he'd be in town tonight, if the girls are dressed for clients, maybe his herd is the one in town.

Men on horseback filled dusty Front Street, whooping, and shooting their guns into the air. Callie covered her nose against the dust and blue smoke in the air and the acrid scent of gunpowder

"They're like a bunch of little boys let out for recess after a long test," Callie said, shaking her chestnut curls.

"All men are little boys at heart and never grow out of it," Lil sighed. "Sometimes I miss all the excitement, though."

"You talk like it was a fun way of life," Callie said

and flinched when more cowboys rushed by shooting their pistols into the air.

"Sugar, on nights like this it could be," Lil said with a broad grin as they stepped into the café, where women moved their skirts aside as they passed. "Stupid bitches," Lil hissed behind Callie.

They took a seat near the back of the room and waited to be noticed by Mr. Jenkins.

It bothers you," Lil said, patting Callie's hand, "the way the good women in this town treat you now. Why?"

Callie exhaled a long breath. "At one time, I thought these women were my friends," Callie sighed. "I just don't understand what I did to deserve this treatment."

"You didn't *do* anything, sugar," Lil sighed and continued to pat Callie's hand. "You're a pretty woman and don't look like you've aged a day past your thirtieth birthday. Now you're without a husband. They see you as a threat to their safe little world," she said and winked.

"If they vilify you in their minds," Lil sighed, "they can justify their poor behavior. These bitches were never your friends, sugar. If they had been, one of them would have invited you into her home when she heard how your husband had dropped you at The Ellsworth."

"I went to church after it all happened," Callie said and brushed a tear from her cheek, "and Deacon Paul asked me to leave. He said I was a tarnished woman now and no longer welcome in the congregation."

"Imagine that," Lil sneered and shrugged her shoulder. "How very Christian of him. Whatever happened to compassion and forgiveness or treating people as you'd have them treat you?"

"What can I get for you ladies this evening?" Mr. Jenkins asked with his usual smile.

"I want some of those chicken and dumplings," Lil told the man, "a cup of coffee and a big piece of pie for dessert."

"I'll have the same," Callie said with a nod.

"What kind of pie?" Mr. Jenkins asked. "We have peach or apple today."

"Whatever empties the pie plate will be fine, sugar," Lil said, and Callie nodded her agreement.

Mr. Jenkins smiled and glanced at the table of chatting women. "I wish all my customers were as agreeable as you ladies from The Ellsworth." With that, he turned and left their table.

"His wife makes a really good pie," Lil said, "Whatever he brings will be tasty."

Callie's eyes went to the door when she heard it open, hoping Clayton would be the one walking in, but each time she'd been disappointed.

I'm acting like a silly schoolgirl.

After the third disappointment, Callie willed herself not to look up and enjoyed her dinner with Lil, whom she found warm and witty. The woman was well read, familiar with Shakespeare, Poe, and a wide range of other authors.

"Books are a fine way to fill your downtime," she'd said when Callie had remarked on her knowledge of literature, "and it's nice to escape into a book every now and again. It's helped to broaden my vocabulary, as well," she added with a grin.

"Mae and Trudy have broadened mine," Callie said and giggled.

"Oh, my," Lil said and rolled her eyes.

As they were finishing their pie, a shadow fell across the table and Callie glanced up to see the handsome sunburned face of Clayton smiling down at her. His silver hair framed his tanned face and his blue eyes shone like sapphires.

"I hoped I might find you here," he said, studying their plates with a mock frown. "Looks like I missed supper, though."

"Nonsense," Callie said nervously with her eyes darting from Clayton to Lil. "Sit down. I'm sure Mrs. Jenkins still has some of her wonderful chicken and dumplings in the kitchen."

"Well," Lil said with a grin, "I think I'll hobble on back home and leave you two young people alone." She stood and patted Callie on the shoulder. "You don't need an old woman here and I need to rinse out some things before I go to bed."

"Good night, Lil," Callie called after the departing woman, who walked slowly without the aid of her cane.

"Lil?" Clayton asked with a raised brow and studied the woman as she left the cafe. "Is she a friend of yours?"

"I guess you could say she is, yes," Callie said with a warm smile on her lips. "She lives at The Ellsworth too."

"Is she a ... I mean does she ..." Clayton stammered uneasily.

"Is she a Soiled Dove?" Callie finished his question with a grin. "She's just an old lady with no place else to go. The Ellsworth is cheap and a good place if you don't have the means to do better."

"You're still there, then?" he asked with a frown.

"It's really not that bad," Callie admitted and took a sip of her cooling coffee.

Clayton's frown deepened. "You shouldn't be living in that place with a bunch of whores," he hissed.

Mr. Jenkins noticed Clayton and came to take his

order. "I'll have what the ladies had and bring her another piece of that pie when you bring mine. She needs more coffee too," the neatly dressed cowboy said, nodding to Callie's empty cup.

Mr. Jenkins walked away shaking his head. "I really shouldn't have more coffee," Callie said. "I'll have a hard enough time getting to sleep tonight as it is."

"Why is that?" Clayton asked with a confused look screwing up his handsome face.

He really is handsome with that big mustache and boyish grin. He's charming too.

"It's your fault, really," Callie said with a grin.

"Mine?" He looked more confused.

"You brought all these rowdy cowboys to town and I'll hear boots tromping up and down the hall all night."

"Oh," he said with a relieved grin. "That bad, is it?"

"You have no idea," Callie said, rolling her eyes as she emptied her cup.

Mr. Jenkins brought coffee and set a plate of chicken and dumplings in front of Clayton. Callie saw other patrons staring at her when they didn't think she was looking. She did her best to ignore them.

Why can't they mind their own damned business?

They talked about Clayton's drive, the weather along the way, and Callie told him about her new business, sewing for the disreputable women in Ellsworth.

"The other seamstresses in town won't sew for them," Callie explained as she sipped her coffee, "so it's a perfect opportunity for me to make some money."

"How much does it pay?" he asked with what Callie thought was genuine interest.

"It depends," Callie said as Mr. Jenkins set plates with slices of peach pie in front of them. "I get a few cents for simple repairs to torn garments and up to two dollars for making a dress, depending on the difficulty of the project. They're keeping me in dinner money," she said and smiled at Mr. Jenkins.

"The women from across the street and other places in Ellsworth patronize The Flat Iron," Mr. Jenkins said, "because the other eateries won't serve them or, like The Palace Hotel, won't even let them in the dining room." He refilled their cups and smiled. "Their money pays the bills just like anyone else's, I say." He patted Callie on the back and walked away shrugging his shoulders.

"Business is business, I suppose," Clayton admitted. "Are you happy with it?"

"I can make more in a week, sewing a few sets of frilly bloomers than I did in a month as a schoolteacher and don't have near the headaches," she told him with a grin tugging at the corners of her mouth.

Clayton took a deep breath. "As much as I hate you living in that horrible place and consorting with those horrible women, I guess you have to do what you have to do to get by."

"Those women are not horrible. Most of them are very nice women just trying to get by," Callie snapped. "Have you ever considered why those women do what they do … how they landed in the situations they're in?" Callie's voice got louder as she continued. "Do you honestly think any of them woke up one morning and said, I think I'll be a whore because it's such a wonderful opportunity for me to get ahead in life?"

Clayton's mind went back to Hawk's story about the Lil he knew in Fredericksburg and frowned.

Could that old lady possibly be her?

He took Callie's flailing hand. "I'm sorry, Callie," he said, quieting her for the moment. "I guess I never really thought about it that way before."

"No," she said, and a weak smile touched her lips, "I'm the one who should be sorry. I shouldn't have lost my temper." Callie gazed around the room. "I'm just tired of people jumping to conclusions about things and people they know nothing about."

They finished their pie with inconsequential chit-chat. Clayton paid for all their dinners, though Callie protested, and they stood to leave. Callie ignored the stares and hooked her arm through Clayton's as they strolled out onto the busy street.

"You're an amazing woman, Callie Jamison," he said as they crossed to the Ellsworth House. He put his arm around her shoulders when he felt her shiver beside him. "Are you cold? Maybe you should have worn a shawl."

"It was warm when Lil and I left," she said and tugged him toward the alley. "I don't want to go through the lobby," Callie said. "Let's go to the back door."

They walked slowly down the narrow alley between The Ellsworth House and the building next door; The Curly Buffalo Saloon. Callie heard piano music and raucous laughter coming from the busy saloon as they passed by.

She stopped at the back door of the Ellsworth and reached for the knob.

"May I kiss you?" Clayton asked, pulling her gently away from the door.

"I suppose," Callie said nervously, gazing up into his steely blue eyes.

Oh, my god, I haven't kissed a man other than Evan in years.

Clayton bent as she lifted her face to his. Their lips met and Callie thought she would faint from the nerves. It had been a very long time. His lips were warm and rough from wind and sunburn, but gentle. He tasted of coffee and peaches when their mouths opened, and their tongues found one another.

Callie didn't know if hers pushed forward first or his, but she didn't care. She relished the moment and allowed him to pull her close and wrap her in his muscular arms. She lifted her hand to caress his neck, twining her fingers in his long, silky hair. Callie breathed in his man-scents—sweat and bay rum after splash.

The kiss lingered longer than it probably should have for proprieties sake, but Callie didn't care. She was a divorced woman and lived in a whorehouse. Polite society didn't see her as a proper woman any longer, anyhow.

She finally broke away and stepped back, breathless with a nervous smile.

Clayton rubbed his chin and grinned. "Now that there was a kiss. How 'bout another?" He pulled her close and Callie didn't resist.

It was the best kiss she'd ever experienced, and she didn't want it to end.

CHAPTER 8
AFTERTHOUGHTS

Clayton had to adjust his trousers as he walked away down the dark alley with a smile spread across his face.

Damn, that was nice. I almost wish she was a whore, so we could have taken it on inside and finished this up.

Too excited to end his night, Clayton stepped into the noisy saloon for a beer to calm him down. The wood-framed building was crowded with men in trousers, clean shirts, and boots. Most were fresh off the trail and ready for a night of drinking and whoring.

Clayton wouldn't get drunk. He wouldn't part with that much of his coin. He wouldn't make use of a whore either for reasons of his own. He stepped up to the bar and edged between two men, who didn't seem to be together and asked the barman for a beer.

"Hey, cowboy," a sweet voice said from behind, "how 'bout you come next door and let me help you with that bulge in your britches." Arms wrapped around Clayton's waist and a feminine hand fell to his crotch to massage his aroused cock.

"I'm sorry, sugar," Clayton said, twisting to

wriggle out of her grasp, "I'm just a poor cowboy. I can't afford the services of a fancy woman like you."

"Then, let me take you out back and suck you, cowboy," she offered with a seductive smile, "that will only cost ya fifty cents instead of a dollar."

"Not tonight," he said sternly. "Move along now."

The bartender pushed a beer past Clayton. "Here ya go, Tabby, look for business on down the bar." He rolled his eyes at Clayton. "Sorry, mister."

"Yah, no problem," he said and tipped up his beer.

Clayton saw Draper and two other crew members at the end of the bar and nodded. He grinned when he saw the young whore with bright strawberry-blonde hair approach the men. He wasn't surprised when the girl whispered something to Danny, the youngest man with the drive. The boy's cheeks blazed red, but he nodded eagerly to the girl, who took his hand and led him from the smoky saloon.

Looks like Danny's gonna be parting with some of his hard-earned coin tonight. I hope it's worth it and he doesn't end up with a case of the French Pox. Riding all the way back to Texas with a fever and a swollen and itching cock won't be any fun.

As Clayton took another sip of his beer, two men stepped up to the bar and ordered a whiskey. They were dressed too well to be cowboys and Clayton took them for local business men from here in Ellsworth.

"What you up to tonight?" the older of the men asked the other as they took their whiskeys.

"Thought I'd find me a woman for a little fun," the younger said and tipped up his glass.

The older man chuckled. "You should go next

door and ask Caine for Callie. She has a few years on her, but her cunny is as sweet as they come."

Clayton suddenly took a closer interest in the conversation.

Is he talking about my Callie? Could there be another?

"Really?" the younger said. "I thought their cunnies dried up when they got old."

"Not this one," the older man assured, "She's as juicy as the day she got popped."

"You poked her?" the younger asked and pushed his glass across the bar for a refill.

"Lots of times," the older man said and emptied his glass. "Give her nipples a good hard twist. She really likes that. She's got the biggest bosoms you'll ever put in your mouth too," the man said with a chuckle. He cupped his hands in front of his chest in imitation of squeezing bosoms. "Damned nice set for an older gal and still firm."

Clayton closed his eyes and trembled with rage.

He is talking about my Callie. She's a damned whore after all. She's not my Callie, she's everybody's Callie. Anybody who'll pay, that is. Just another lying, filthy whore.

Clayton emptied his mug and slammed it down on the bar.

I gotta get the hell out of this whore-ridden town.

He dropped a coin on the bar, pushed away, and stormed out of the saloon.

What Clayton didn't hear:

"Wait a minute, Jamison," the younger man scoffed, "isn't your wife's name Callie?"

"She's not my wife anymore," the older man said, slurring his speech from too many whiskeys. "I've been shed of her for months, now and couldn't be happier. She's living at The Ellsworth with the rest of the tramps in this damned town." He chuckled loudly and downed another glass of whiskey.

CHAPTER 9
WHAT DID I DO NOW?

It had been three days since her dinner with Clayton and their kiss. He hadn't been back to town, leaving Callie confused. He'd told her he'd meet her the next night at the Flat Iron, but Callie had waited in the café until nine. He hadn't come, though his men were still in town and visiting the girls.

Maybe he got called away. Maybe he just didn't like the kiss. He said it was a nice kiss, though.

Callie busied herself with her sewing and tried to keep her mind off Clayton and the amazing kiss. She would never understand the minds of men.

What the hell do they want? What do they expect from a woman? Am I simply supposed to sit here on the edge of my seat, and wait until he reappears from God knows where?

Callie pricked her finger with the sharp needle. "Shit," she gasped and stuck the injured finger into her mouth before the tiny drops of blood could mar the white fabric she was making a dressing gown from.

Someone knocked. "Come in," she called and set the sewing aside. It was probably Mae coming to check on her progress.

The door opened and Caine strolled in. He closed the door behind him, locked it, and tossed the key onto the bed.

"What the hell do you want?" Callie snapped and jumped to her feet.

"What … I … want," Caine growled as he stepped toward her, "is what's due me."

He reached out for Callie, but she stepped aside. "Hasn't Evan been paying the rent?" she sneered. "If not, you should take it up with Judge Sterling. He's the one who ordered Evan to pay my rent."

Caine chuckled, but the look Callie saw in his dark eyes was anything but mirthful.

"You know?" he said, looming over her. "I've watched you in town for years, Mrs. Callie Jamison, respectable, churchgoing wife and schoolteacher." He took another step. "You didn't, did you? No, of course not." He took another step. "You wouldn't give a man like me a second look, would you?"

"I was a married woman. I wasn't in the habit of noticing other men," Callie protested and stepped back. Her back bounced against the wall.

"Yes," he sneered, "your husband. What a piece of work that one is." Caine leered down at her. "He sold you to me, you know. He sold you like a piece of meat in a butcher's shop."

"What?" Callie gasped.

He's deranged. I've got to get out of here.

"I gave him a twenty-dollar gold for you," Caine said and moved closer. "You are my property now and I demand to have what I paid for." He made a quick step forward and grabbed Callie's arm. "I think I'll have it now if you please," Caine said and pulled her into his chest.

"You can't *buy* people anymore," Callie hissed as

she glared up at Caine. "A war was fought over it. Remember?"

Callie attempted to push away from him, but he held firm to her upper arm. "The niggers might be free," he said coolly, staring into her eyes, "but a white woman is still her husband's property to do with as he pleases." He chuckled maniacally and took hold of Callie's trembling chin. "And Evan Jamison sold you to me for a twenty-dollar gold piece."

He held her chin tightly in his hand. She would have bruises tomorrow. "And just what do you want of me?" Callie sneered through clenched teeth. "Do you want what's due a husband from a wife? Love? Honor? Obedience?" Callie had thought long and hard about what she would do should Caine assault her again.

I've had about enough of this stupid son-of-a-bitch.

"I want my twenty-dollars-worth," he spat and ran his hand down her throat to her heaving bosoms. He brushed the right one until her nipple hardened and he began applying pressure with a grin on his scarred face.

"Twenty pokes, then?" Callie asked and took a deep breath. She pressed her bosoms into Caine boldly. "One a day for twenty days or two a day for ten?" she sneered.

"Don't know about that," he said as he pulled the pins from her hair, "but I think I want the first one now." He began fingering the buttons on her dress.

"Don't," Callie hissed and slapped at Caine's fumbling hand. "I'll do it. I hate stitching buttons back on and resewing the slits."

Callie began popping open the buttons one at a time, allowing the dress to fall open inch-by-inch until her frilly, white cotton camisole was exposed.

She repeated the process with the buttons on the camisole until her full bosoms fell out in plain sight.

Caine stood, staring wide-eyed as she shrugged out of the dress and let it fall to the floor. She pushed the camisole from her shoulders, and it dropped to join the dress. Callie ran her hands over her bosoms and pinched each hard nipple provocatively.

Callie watched Caine shudder as she pulled the ribbon holding her petticoat up, loosed the waist, and let it fall to puddle at her feet with the discarded dress. She stood stiff-backed and naked before Caine, thrusting her bosoms forward. Callie took in the dumbfounded expression on the man's face and ran one of her hands through the tangle of hair between her naked thighs.

Caine trembled and took short deep breaths as he watched her.

"Come on, big man," she whispered as she reached for his bulging trousers, "show me what you have in there for me."

He slapped her hand aside, turned and stormed to the door. When he turned back, Callie tossed him the key. She'd dropped onto the bed in a sultry pose with her legs partially spread. She wanted him to see her with her finger inside.

"Damned slut," he cursed as he yanked the door open and threw himself into the hall.

Callie jumped from the bed, ran to the door, and locked it. Her heart thudded as she leaned against the wood and slid to the floor.

Damn. I was taking a chance with that little show, but I'm glad I was right about the big bastard.

During one of their discussions concerning men and the business of pleasuring them, Mae had told Callie how some men could only enjoy a woman if he dominated her. They enjoyed beating and demeaning a woman with filthy slurs and violence. They were unable to perform in any other situation with a woman. Callie had suspected Caine to be one of those men.

Thank the lord I was right. What would I have done if he'd undone those damned trousers?

Callie rose unsteadily from the floor after her heart stopped pounding. She slipped into her dressing gown and pulled the tie tight at the front. From a drawer in her wardrobe, Callie took out a loaf of bread purchased at the bakery and a crock of peach preserves. She cut a slice off the crusty loaf and slathered it with jam. She needed something in her stomach.

She'd taken to buying a little food to keep in her room. Mae had told her all the women did it. Most had small stoves in their rooms as well for heat in the winter and for making coffee. Callie intended to look into buying one. Winter would be upon them soon and she surely missed her morning coffee.

Callie dropped into her chair and bit into the bread. The sweet taste of peach preserves filled her mouth as she chewed. She thought about what had just happened with Caine and shivered. Callie smiled as she bit into the bread again, proud of the fact she'd handled the situation to her advantage.

I'm going to have to watch my back now, though. I don't think Caine is the forgiving sort. He thinks I owe him twenty dollars and he wants to take it out of my hide. What the hell do I do now?

CHAPTER 10
CONTEMPLATION

C layton led Dolly to the wide, clear stream and stood watching as the big mare drank her fill. He patted her flank.

"What are we gonna do now, Dolly? Back to Texas for the winter or take a chance here in Kansas?" Clayton sighed and tried to clear his head.

He'd been riding in circles for weeks. The cattle season had ended. There would be no drives until the spring. Clayton had ridden as far as the Nations before turning around and riding back toward Kansas.

What the hell am I doing? She's just another damned whore. Beautiful and articulate, but still a whore. When I left Fredericksburg all those years ago, I swore I was done with whores.

Dolly seemed to be finished, so Clayton took her reins and led her back to the grass.

"Let's rest here for a bit, Dolly," Clayton said to the mare as he slipped the bit from her mouth. "This looks like a nice place."

He took the saddle from the mare's back and carried it closer to the stream and a flat, grassy spot.

Clayton rolled out his blankets before building a small fire.

This near the water, the predators might come close in the night. He fed the tiny fire until the flames danced in the night. He collected more wood from along the stream and piled it beside the pit he'd dug.

The warmth coming off the fire as he lounged on his blankets reminded Clayton of the warmth he'd felt radiating off Callie's body as they'd stood kissing. It had been a wonderful kiss … the best kiss he'd ever had. He suddenly sat up and stared into the flames.

She kissed me. That's something most whores don't do … they don't kiss their clients. It's like a universal whore rule … no kissing, especially with tongues. She kissed me, though. She kissed me and it was one hell of a goddamned kiss.

Clayton fell back on his bedroll with his head resting on his saddle. He fell asleep with a smile on his face and an easing of his troubled mind about the pretty woman.

⚜

THE WARM SUN on his face woke Clayton from the first sound sleep he'd had in weeks. He squinted as he rolled out of his blankets, stood, and walked to a clump of bushes to relieve himself. From his saddlebags, Clayton took his coffee pot. He pulled on his boots and went to the stream for water.

I think better with coffee in my belly.

As he sat, sipping his first cup of coffee, Clayton saw something in the distance he hadn't noticed yesterday when he'd stopped by this stream. He rubbed his eyes. It looked to be a small homestead with a house and a barn. He didn't see any movement—no people or stock.

Clayton continued to study the homestead while

he finished his coffee. The land from where he sat to the buildings was flat and lush. The stream appeared to him to be one that flowed year-round. That would be a boon to any homestead.

I wonder why there are no horses or cattle grazing in this field. I think I'll go ask.

Clayton cleaned his pot in the stream, cleared his camp, and stowed his gear.

"Come on, Dolly," Clayton said as he led the horse back to the stream.

While the mare drank, Clayton secured the saddle to her back. "Let's go have a look and see what's up with that homestead." He got in the saddle and urged the mare across the grassy field.

The dry ryegrass swayed in the breeze. Occasional clumps of yellow goldenrod stood tall and unmoving along with thorny, creeping dewberry vines.

No stock has grazed in this field in a very long time—if ever.

As he drew nearer, Clayton could tell the homestead had been abandoned. A sturdy barn stood at the back of the property with roughly an acre fenced for stock though none stood in the weedy pasture.

Between the barn and the house, Clayton saw a small area surrounded by white pickets and he frowned. He turned Dolly and rode toward the pickets. Within were two mounds—one large and one small. Wooden slabs had been planted at the head of both. They read Jane Coventry b. 1843 d. 1873 and James Coventry Jr. b. 1873 d. 1873.

Clayton removed his hat in reverence and bowed his head with a sad frown. This wasn't the first private burial site he'd seen in his travels. Women and their babies died out here on the prairie all too often.

He returned his hat to his head and nudged Dolly toward the house. He saw two posts with line strung between—a clothesline. Nearby stood a wood-framed well with a bucket and crank under a roof. A covered porch stretched along a quarter of the building. Windows with glass and storm shutters dotted the sturdy structure. The remnants of a garden patch fenced with more pickets against rabbits lie behind the line along with an outhouse, an empty chicken coop, and another small shed.

Somebody spent some coin building up this place. Glass windows way out here are uncommon. He spent some on that milled lumber he sided it with too. I bet he was an easterner who sold out and came west with high hopes of a bright future and a pocket full of coin.

Clayton's curiosity had been piqued. He tied Dolly to a hitching post at the front of the tidy lap-sided house and stepped up onto the front porch. A swing hung with chain from the porch ceiling squeaked in the early morning breeze.

He turned the knob on the door, pushed it open, and stepped inside. The rooms were in disarray, but not empty. In the front parlor, a lone red velvet settee stood with a matching footstool in front of it and a side table.

Clayton walked past it into a kitchen with empty shelves and a lone wood cook stove. It was as if the former inhabitants had simply walked away one day, leaving whatever wouldn't fit into their wagon.

On either end of the house were large bedrooms. Inside one Clayton found an ornate cradle and a narrow bed. This had been a child's room. He opened the hand-hewn wardrobe and found a variety of infant's garments. He suspected the owner of the garments now lies in one of the graves in the back.

With trepidation, Clayton wandered into the other bedroom. Another bed stood in the room. Like the one in the child's room, the bed was neatly made, covered with a carefully stitched quilt. Curtains made of yellowed lace hung at the windows. Clayton pulled them open to allow sunshine to illuminate the room. As he suspected, Clayton found a woman's clothes hanging in the wardrobe.

The man, James Coventry Sr., Clayton assumed, had walked away, and left his wife and his child here, along with all their personal belongings. Clayton wondered if he had been able to leave their memories behind as well.

As he was about to leave the sad room, Clayton spotted a piece of paper pinned to one of the pillows. He unpinned it and carried it to the window for the light.

To you who find this note,

My one remaining son and I are giving up on this place and returning to Ohio where we came from and where we should have stayed. This venture was Jane's dream, not mine, and she's gone now along with my other son. We worked hard together to build this farm. You'll find the buildings sturdy and the ground fruitful. I only ask that you tend the graves of my dear wife and son and treat them with respect.
We homesteaded this land. It's registered at the courthouse in Ellsworth in the name of James Allen Coventry. I've been told you can use this letter as a transfer of deed on the land. It is a full six-hundred-forty-acre homestead. It has been improved with a house and barn and we were here for a full five years. The land is mine to transfer, though they may ask for back-taxes.

I wish you well here. It's brought me nothing but grief.

James Allen Coventry Sr. 5 July 1873

CLAYTON CARRIED the note back to the parlor and dropped onto the settee. He read it again as he peered around the vacant room. A massive fieldstone fireplace stood on the wall between the parlor and the kitchen. The kitchen stove stood with the flue pipe set into it on the other side. James Coventry had been a fine builder.

Maybe I've found my shelter for the winter and my retirement from the cowboy life.

He carefully folded James Coventry's letter and put it in his pocket. He'd go into Ellsworth tomorrow and do what he must to transfer Coventry's claim into his name. Clayton hoped it wouldn't have to involve a lawyer. He hated lawyers.

Clayton stepped outside, untied Dolly, and walked with her to the barn. "I think this is gonna be home for a spell, Dolly," he said as he took the bit out of the big mare's mouth. He opened the gate to the fenced pasture and Dolly went through unbidden and began munching on the tall, green grass. "What ya think, girl?" he called as he hooked the gate. The red mare lifted her head, huffed loudly, and pawed at the grassy ground.

"That's what I think too," he said with a smile and walked toward the barn.

He unhooked the door and pulled one of the big double-doors open. The scent of moldy hay and cow hit Clayton's nose as soon as he entered the sturdy barn. Inside, Clayton saw lofts on both sides above him and well-built stalls below. One had a yoke for a milk cow. In a corner, Clayton saw a forge for shoeing horses.

This is a great barn. It's an excellent start for a little farm, if not a ranch.

After taking in the barn, Clayton took a walk around the property. He located one marker stake and walked in the direction he thought the next one would be found. It took Clayton three hours to walk the property and find the other three stakes. He found a stand of woods composed of oak, hickory, and sweetgums. It stood not far from the house, but Clayton would require a wagon to transport firewood to the house.

He also walked around a small stock pond and hoped it had fish. His walk scared up two fat rabbits as well as a sleek whitetail and a covey of quail.

At least I know there's game on the property. Maybe I'll go hunting tomorrow. A nice fat rabbit would be good for supper.

Clayton dropped the load of firewood he'd collected along the way back by the door and took a seat in the porch swing. He sat back and stared off across the field in front of the house. Tall burnt-orange grasses swayed in the breeze. He imagined what it would look like green in the summer.

I have a house, a potentially productive ranch, and a place to rest my old bones. Now I just need that woman to keep me warm at night.

He walked back to the barn and collected his rucksack containing his cooking supplies from his saddlebags. Clayton thought about Callie again as he built a fire in the cast-iron stove. He wondered if she could cook. His mother had been a good cook. Clayton went to the well and brought up a bucket of water. He tested it and found the water sweet. Inside, he put on a pot of coffee.

This place could certainly use a woman's touch.

CHAPTER 11
A WOMAN'S TOUCH

"What can I get for ya, Mr. Caine?" the bartender at the Curly Buffalo Saloon asked.

"Gi' me a beer," Caine growled.

"You got it," the bartender said and turned around for a mug.

"Hey there, Caine," Evan Jamison said and slapped the big man on the back. "Got that bitch wife of mine sucking cock over there yet?" he asked with a chuckle.

Caine turned his head and frowned. "I didn't want her for that, Evan."

"With all that sweet, young cunny prancing around The Ellsworth," Evan said with a grin, "you wanted Callie's old dried up one?"

"She's a very handsome woman," Caine said. "She's better than any of those young whores."

"Callie hasn't been cooperative yet? You haven't been able to slip in between her sheets and have your way?" Evan asked with a raised brow. "I'm sure if you keep after her, she'll finally give in. Now that she's lost her silly job, I'm sure you can persuade her with a little coin from time to time or maybe a dinner at The Flat Iron."

"Callie," Caine said as he sipped his beer, "has no need of my coin. She's making her own."

"She's taking customers?" Evan asked wide-eyed. "She must be more desperate than I thought."

"She's no whore," Caine snapped. "She's taking in sewing from the girls and making clothes for them."

"She was always good at that," Evan admitted.

"I don't understand why you wanted to put her aside."

Evan slapped Caine's back and chuckled. "You of all men should know why. I want something younger and fresher, someone, who can give me the son I need. Callie has been incapable of doing her duty in that regard," Evan sighed and gulped down his shot of whiskey. "The only thing she's good for now is poking, so, I'll leave her to you." Evan pushed the glass across the bar for a refill. "If you can't persuade her gently, then use your fists. It always worked for me."

⁂

CALLIE STROLLED DOWN the boardwalk toward the mercantile. She needed some ribbon and lace to finish her current project. As she came upon the Butterfield depot, someone came stumbling out into her path. Callie stopped before colliding with the person carrying two heavy leather cases.

"Oh, I'm ..." Polly Hardin stopped in mid-apology to glare at Callie. "I didn't see you," she hissed.

"Obviously," Callie said as she tried to step around the glaring girl who was dressed for traveling in a conservative dark suit and straw bonnet.

"Why'd you have to go and ruin my life, Callie?" the girl called after her.

Callie turned in dismay. "Ruin *your* life?" Callie snapped and took a step back toward the girl. "How do you figure *I* ruined *your* life, young lady? I am the injured party here. I was a married woman with a home and a respectable job until some greedy little tart started rolling in the bushes with my husband."

"Evan just wants a child," Polly said with a quivering lower lip. "I can give him one," she said with a hand moving to her belly, "and you can't."

"So, I heard," Callie retorted. "I'm surprised there hasn't been a wedding yet."

Callie saw tears welling in the girl's big brown eyes. "There's not going to be one," Polly whispered.

"Oh?" Callie said in surprise. "And why is that?"

Polly's eyes narrowed again, and she brushed the tears from her cheeks with her gloved hand.

"You made it sound to the Martins," Polly hissed, "that I'd had other lovers and … and Evan refused to marry me. I lost my opportunity to teach at the school, and Papa is so upset with me, he's sending me off to St. Louis to live with my aunt until the baby comes." Polly took a deep, sobbing breath. "He says I have to give it up to a foundling home there or I can't come back to Ellsworth."

Callie suddenly felt sorry for the sobbing girl she'd known and taught for seven years. She took the girl into her arms. "I'm sorry, Polly," she whispered. "I truly am."

"I'm sorry too, Mrs. Jamison," Polly sobbed on Callie's shoulder, "I never meant for any of this to happen."

I'm sure you didn't. Evan Jamison, you are such an ass. How can you just turn your back on this child when she's prob-

ably carrying that precious son you've been begging for all these years?

Callie took the girl by the shoulders and gave her a little shake. "But it has happened, Polly and now we both must deal with it." She stared the wide-eyed girl in the face. "Do you really want to come back to Ellsworth? There's not going to be much for you here now, is there?"

Polly shook her head. "No, ma'am, not now that my reputation's been ruined."

Well, that's certainly not my fault. Stupid girl.

"You're an educated girl, Polly. I'm sure you will find more opportunities in St. Louis than here in Ellsworth. Do you think your aunt would help you?

Polly snorted. "I know she would. She hates my papa. He called her a whore because she got with child when she was my age and kept her baby." More tears slid down Polly's cheeks. "Papa says we're two of a kind and have shamed the Hardin name."

"And let him without sin cast the first stone," Callie sighed.

"What do you mean by that?" Polly hiccupped.

You never were very good at math, Polly.

"You were born in July. Were you not?" Callie asked.

"Yes."

"And when were your parents married?"

"They had a Christmas wedding," Polly said before her mouth dropped open. "They were married in December before I was born."

"Exactly," Callie sighed. "Your mother was at least two months along with you when they got married."

"What a sanctimonious son-of-a-bitch," Polly hissed.

Both women turned as the stage pulled up to the

depot. Polly waited for the passengers to disembark, handed the driver her ticket and bags, and hugged Callie tentatively before stepping up into the rig.

"Thank you, Mrs. Jamison," Polly said.

"Good luck to you, Polly," Callie said and waved to the sad-eyed girl before walking on toward Martin's Mercantile.

"What can I get for you today?" Mr. Martin asked without looking Callie in the eye.

If I had any other choice, I wouldn't be shopping here at all, but I don't.

"I need three yards of that four-inch white machined lace, please, a spool of white thread, and a yard of white satin ribbon."

Mr. Martin pulled the lace from the spool to measure it. "I only have four yards left on this spool," he said with a forced smile. "I'll let you have it for five cents a yard if you take it all."

How generous, a whole penny a yard off the price.

"Certainly," Callie said as she strolled past him to examine a display of stoves nearby as he collected her needles, thread, and ribbon. She read the tag hanging from the handle of a small iron potbelly: Three dollars including stove pipe and installation.

Callie rolled her eyes. Three dollars amounted to what her entire month's salary teaching at the school had been.

There was frost on the branches outside my window this morning. I suppose it's time to start thinking on one of these and hot coffee in my room would surely be nice.

"I'll have this as well," she said, indicating the stove.

"Do you have a room with a flue or an outside wall?" Mr. Martin asked from behind the counter.

"What's the difference?" Callie asked.

"If it must go through an outside wall, I have to

charge you for the outside chimney pipe. It's an extra twenty-five cents."

Callie thought about it and supposed it made sense. "An extra twenty-five cents it is, then. When can you deliver and install it?"

"I think I can work it into my delivery schedule for tomorrow," he said without looking up, "but it must be early in the day. The missus and I are going to the dance tomorrow night."

"Of course," Callie said. "I'll have my room ready after nine in the morning. Is that early enough?"

He nodded, scratched on a receipt book with his pencil, and said, "That will be three dollars and forty-five cents for the lace, the notions, the stove, and the extra flue pipe. Can I interest you in an ash bucket or poker?" It irked Callie that the man wouldn't look her in the face.

What an ass.

"Not today," Callie declined. "Perhaps next time." She paid for her purchase and took the bundle. "I'm in room one-o-one," Callie added before stepping out of the store into the crisp autumn afternoon.

I forgot about the damned dance. I told Mae and Trudy I'd go with them to the silly thing.

Callie hurried across the street and up the boardwalk to the Ellsworth House.

"Is my new dressing gown finished yet?" Tabby asked as Callie stepped into the lobby.

"I have to gather the lace and sew it onto the last sleeve," she said, holding up the folded bundle of lace. "Give me half an hour." Callie gave the strawberry-blonde girl a crooked smile. "You're not going to be needing it tonight anyway."

"But," Tabby said wide-eyed, "I wanted to wear

it tonight. It's getting too cold to lounge around in this drafty lobby in just my bloomers and camisole." She gave Callie a grin and a wink. "I'll catch my death."

"Mr. Martin will be delivering a stove to my room in the morning," she told Caine as she passed him standing in his place behind the counter.

"You should have asked permission for that," Caine growled.

"And you should provide heat in your damned rented rooms," Callie snapped back. "I think I'll write a letter to the governor about it. I'm sure it's a cause the Progressives would like to take up in the State Senate. Landlords forcing their tenants in a boarding house to supply their own stoves is absolutely ridiculous."

"Here, here," one girl called from the settees. "You tell the cheap bastard, Callie," chimed in another while the others in the room giggled.

"Troublemaking bitch," Caine snarled as Callie walked on to her room. "You, lazy cunnies would keep plenty warm if you were doing your jobs the way you should."

Callie ignored the crude comments the women hurled at Caine and returned to her room where she went back to work on Tabby's dressing gown.

After finishing, she went to her wardrobe and took out the dress she'd been working on for herself. In her spare time, Callie had taken apart the blue velvet dress Lil had brought her. It had been an outdated style with a very full skirt to fit over hoops, full sleeves, and an off the shoulder collar. The narrow waist told Callie Lil hadn't wedged herself into the dress in quite some time.

Callie had removed the skirt, cut it down by taking out several sections, and reattached it with a stylish apron and a large lace-trimmed bow at the rear. She cut new sleeves to replace the outdated full ones. Pretty lace inset at the neckline added some modesty to the tight, boned bodice. Callie enjoyed creating new garments from old ones.

If I can get this finished, maybe I can wear it to the silly dance tomorrow night.

As the natural light faded, Callie lit her lamp. She stitched into the night and her mind wandered to Clayton and their kiss again. It had been weeks now and she'd received no letters from the man. She couldn't understand it. Had she done something wrong? Did he think less of her because she'd let him kiss her?

Men are such unfathomable creatures.

Was he upset that she hadn't moved out of The Ellsworth House? And move where? The Palmer Hotel? She couldn't afford a dollar a day at the Palmer. There was Mrs. Finch's Boarding house, but she really couldn't afford that either and Callie was certain Evan wouldn't agree to the relocation.

Maybe I should have gone to Judge Sterling after what Caine said about Evan making some sort of deal with him, but I'm sure the judge wouldn't have believed me. Hell, they may have all been in on it together. Just one big laugh at my expense.

Evan said he was setting me aside to marry Polly because she was carrying the son he hoped for. Now he's set her aside too. What's he up to?

"I'll never fathom the minds of men. They're all a basket of bad apples."

CHAPTER 12

THE SILLY DANCE

"How do I look?" Mae asked for the dozenth time as she adjusted a pin in her hair and dabbed rouge on her pouty, pink lips.

"You look beautiful," Callie assured the girl. "Now will you go on, so I can finish getting dressed?"

"Oh, very well," the redhead huffed. "Don't you want me to wait, so I can hook you in the back?" The girl glanced at Callie's newly installed stove and smiled. "I guess you can have coffee in the mornings now."

"Yes, thank God," Callie sighed. "Now all I need is wood for a fire, a pot, and coffee. I guess I have to make another trip to the damned mercantile."

"You'll need a cup too," Mae said with a grin. "I'll have Sam come by the next time I see him. He delivers wood and takes out ashes for us girls. He only charges fifteen cents a month." Mae's green eyes darted to the wardrobe. "You ready to put that dress on yet?"

"All right," Callie conceded, knowing the girl wanted to get the first look at Callie's new party dress.

Callie took the sapphire-blue velvet garment

from the hanger in her wardrobe and stepped into it. She pulled it up over her white petticoat and slid her arms into the sleeves.

"This is so pretty," Mae gushed as she hooked the bodice in the back over Callie's tightly laced corset and ran her hand down the velvet skirt.

Callie had to admit as she tied the apron in the back, the bright white lace contrasting against the jewel-toned blue velvet looked amazing as she admired the dress in the mirror on her wardrobe door.

Mae had brushed Callie's auburn curls up and secured them with a white satin ribbon and pins. A few stray curls hung provocatively in front of each ear and down the nape of her neck. Callie pinned a Wedgewood-blue cameo brooch at her throat and then slipped her hands into a pair of white gloves.

She twirled in front of the wardrobe. "How do *I* look?" Callie asked her young friend.

"Stunning," Mae said wide-eyed. "Absolutely stunning."

Mae tossed Callie her bag and rushed her out of the door. Mae locked the door, handed Callie the key, and took her hand to pull her into the lobby.

"What do you think, ladies?" Mae asked, presenting Callie to the women lounging there.

Callie heard admiring gasps from the women. "Did you make that from that old gown I brought you?" Lil asked and rose from her seat to admire Callie's repurposed garment. "This is amazing," she said with a wink. "Maybe I want it back."

"As if you could fit your fat old ass in it now," one of the women said with a chuckle.

"Come on, Trudy," Mae urged her blonde friend, "we're gonna miss the first dance if we don't get going."

"What are you gawking at?" Trudy asked Caine, who stood staring at Callie, open-mouthed.

"You have your cunnies back here as soon as that damned dance is over," he scolded. "There will be plenty of hard cocks here looking for some release tonight and I want you all here." He gave Callie a grin. "Now, get on down there and show 'em what they've got to look forward to later."

Trudy rolled her big blue eyes as Mae tugged Callie out the door. "Come on, Callie. You're gonna make all those townie wives so jealous in that dress."

"I'm afraid I have to agree with her on that," Trudy sighed. "It's really beautiful and nobody else is gonna be wearing anything like it."

"You don't think it's too revealing, do you?" Callie asked, brushing her hand over the lace covering her bosoms, bulging from the top of her tight corset.

"You're asking us?" Trudy cackled.

"Point taken," Callie sighed and continued down the boardwalk toward the barn where music, a crowd of buggies, and light announced the location of Ellsworth's Harvest Festival Dance.

At the door, Mae and Trudy rushed in and were soon lost in the crush of bodies.

How did I let them talk me into this?

"Buy you a drink, ma'am?" Callie jerked her head up to see the steel-blue eyes of Clayton Swift smiling down at her.

"A sarsaparilla would be most welcome," she said with a smile.

Clayton took her arm and led her to a table where a man stood tapping drinks into mugs from wooden barrels. "A sarsaparilla for the lady and a beer for me, please," Clayton said.

The man filled the mugs and handed them the drinks. "That'll be ten cents."

"Here ya go," Clayton said and handed the man a silver coin. "Shall we find a seat and watch? I'm afraid I'm not much of one for dancing."

Callie smiled up at him uneasily. "That sounds fine. I'm not much of a dancer either."

"I thought all women liked to dance," he said with a sheepish grin as he led her through the crowd to an empty bench.

Callie smiled. "I think we all like to dance," she said and nodded to the dancefloor where a rotund woman in pink jerked her partner around the floor like a bird dog with a limp quail. "I didn't say we were all much good at it."

Clayton smiled and tipped up his beer. He used his sleeve to wipe the foam from his bushy gray mustache.

"How have you been?" he asked.

"Busy," she replied with a sigh. "I got three more orders this week for dressing gowns." Callie turned her head to watch Mae and Trudy dancing together. "Mae's a fantastic saleswoman."

"I bet she is," Clayton said with a frown. "She looks to be selling herself tonight."

Callie sipped her sarsaparilla to hide her displeasure with his remark. "She's a sweet girl," Callie said as she watched the young redhead on the dancefloor. "But she's really just a girl."

"If you say so," Clayton huffed but avoided Callie's eyes.

"What is your problem with women?" Callie snapped.

"Not women," he sighed, "just whores."

"Is there a story here?" Callie asked.

"Yah, I suppose there is." He sipped his beer again but didn't say more.

"Where have you been?" Callie asked after a long silence.

Clayton shifted his eyes to stare at Callie.

Damn, she's beautiful, but she's a whore. Just look what she's wearing ... all that lace and velvet with her bosoms barely hidden—a whore's dress.

"I've been around."

"You didn't write," Callie whispered before taking another drink.

"Nope."

"Well, okay," Callie said, drained her mug, and stood. "I guess I'll see you when I see you."

"Wait a minute," Clayton said and grabbed her wrist.

"Yes?" She turned to glare at him.

"Don't leave," he begged and dropped her wrist. "I'm sorry." He dropped back into his seat and motioned toward the empty bench. "Please sit and talk with me."

Callie sat again. "I don't understand what's going on," Callie sighed. "Did I do something to upset you?" She waited for an answer, but he simply stared at the dancers. "I waited at The Flat Iron, but you never came. What happened?"

"I ... I ... had to think about things," he stammered. "I needed to clear my head."

"About me?" she asked hesitantly. "About us?"

"Yah," he sighed and emptied his beer. "I needed to sort some things out in my head."

Callie took a deep nervous breath. "And did you? Sort things out?"

"I did," he said and stood. "Can I get you another?" He lifted his empty mug.

"Sure," she said and handed him hers. She watched him walk away.

What am I supposed to think about all of this? He's so damned handsome and writes such sweet letters, but he can't explain himself. He had things to sort out? What things?

"I can't believe you have the nerve to show your face here."

Callie jerked her head up to see the angry, red face of Calvin Hardin glaring down at her with his wife, Vivian, standing by his side.

"Why wouldn't I?" Callie retorted. "It's a community event open to the public."

"You ruined my daughter's good name," he hissed loud enough to attract the attention of people sitting nearby.

Callie rolled her eyes. "I think you should be talking to Evan about that," Callie jabbed back. "I had nothing to do with getting her into her condition."

Hardin pointed his finger in Callie's face. "But you're the one who announced it to the whole damned town in The Flat Iron."

"I think," Callie said and stood, "that the whole damned town was going to find out about it eventually without my input."

"But ... but ... you made it sound like she was ... was ..." Vivian Hardin said, stepping up beside her husband to glare down at Callie. "You shouldn't have done that, Callie."

"No," Callie said with an embarrassed sigh, "I shouldn't have done that, but I was angry ... at Evan, at Polly, and at the Martins." She raised her hands. "I'd just lost my marriage because of Polly and then I found out I was losing my job and Polly was trying to take it."

"And you blamed my daughter for that?" Calvin

shouted. "You couldn't keep your man at home, and you had to embarrass my little girl in public, calling her a common whore in front of everyone?"

"Again," Callie said and took a step back, "you should be angry at Evan for despoiling *your little girl,* and not me."

"If you'd been taking care of your husband," Calvin seethed, "he wouldn't have been looking for comfort outside of his marriage."

"What's going on here?" Clayton asked as he walked back holding two mugs in his hands.

"It's nothing," Callie said. "These are my former neighbors and they were just saying hello."

"This isn't over, schoolteacher," Calvin yelled as Vivian tugged at his arm, red-faced. "You're done in this town. I'll see to it."

"Oh, my," Callie said and took a long gulp of her sarsaparilla.

"What was that all about?" Clayton asked as he sat. "It didn't look to me like a simple hello from neighbors."

Callie went on to explain the situation with Polly Hardin, her former student, Evan, her former husband, and her former position at the school.

"Hardin and your husband sound like a pair," Clayton said. "I feel sorry for that poor girl."

"So, do I," Callie sighed and emptied her glass. "I think I should be going now. It's getting late."

"May I walk you home?" he asked and took her hand in his.

"I suppose," she said hesitantly and stood.

They left the dance hand-in-hand and walked down the quiet street toward The Ellsworth House.

"Would you like to go for a buggy ride tomorrow?" he asked when they got to the back door.

"I think that would be lovely," she replied with a smile.

Clayton, bolstered by her positive reply, took Callie's face in his hand, bent, and kissed her passionately on her soft, warm lips.

"You're an amazing woman, Callie," he whispered between kisses and eased her back against the door. "I want more than just kisses."

The ardent kisses had ignited a flame in Callie. Her nipples hardened and throbbed along with the spot between her thighs.

You're not the only one, cowboy, but it wouldn't be proper.

"So, do I, Clayton, but not here. I can't bring you into my room. It wouldn't be proper."

Clayton kissed her again. "I understand," he sighed. "I'll pick you up in the morning about nine?"

Callie gazed up into his smiling eyes. "That sounds fine," she said with an uneasy smile.

"See you then," he said, turned, and walked off down the alley.

Now we'll see if he actually shows up or if he ends up with more things to sort out.

CHAPTER 13
IT WOULDN'T BE PROPER

C allie was pleasantly surprised when a buggy stopped in front of the Ellsworth House promptly at nine. She waited out front, not wanting to offend Clayton with the women inside. A heavy crocheted shawl covered her warm, blue chintz day dress and she had gloves on her hands against the October chill.

"I would have come inside to get you, like a proper gentleman," he said when she stepped up into the buggy.

"I didn't want you to be uncomfortable in the house," she said as she arranged her skirts in the seat. "I could use the fresh air, anyhow."

"Have you eaten breakfast?" Clayton asked as he took the reins.

Callie snorted. "There are no kitchens in the rooms at the Ellsworth."

Clayton smiled and turned the buggy around in the street. "Let's eat then." He brought the horse to a halt outside The Flat Iron. He jumped down, secured the buggy's weight, and took Callie's chintz-clad arm.

Inside the busy café, Mr. Jenkins waved as they

took a seat by the window. Callie's mouth watered as the aromas of brewing coffee, frying bacon, onions, and hot biscuits filled her nose.

Damn, it's been a long time since I sat down to a hot breakfast.

Callie worked her gloves off as Mr. Jenkins brought cups and a pot of coffee to their table. "What can I get you, folks, today?" he asked with his usual cordial smile.

"I want two eggs yolky," Callie said, "bacon, and biscuits with butter."

It smells so damn good in here.

"I'll have the same," Clayton said with a broad grin creasing his handsome face. "You must be hungry."

"I haven't eaten since some bread and jam yesterday afternoon," Callie admitted.

Clayton's eyes went wide. "You should have said something last night at the dance. I'd have taken you to supper or at least bought you a muffin to go with the sarsaparilla."

Callie waved him off. "I was fine… last night, but I could surely eat a horse this morning."

"I can't believe there are no ways for you girls to make food in your rooms," Clayton said and sipped his coffee.

"I have a stove in my room now," Callie said with a raised brow. "Now I can at least make coffee and warm some bread when I want to."

"And warm your behind," he said and grinned. "The first snow will fly soon."

"I know," Callie said. "It's already cold in the mornings with frost on the window glass."

"And the nights," he said.

Callie's brow furrowed with concern. "Have you been sleeping outside on the cold ground?"

"My old hide is tough," he said, "I'm getting along."

"I'm glad," Callie said and smiled.

My God, that smile is beautiful. I think I could look at it every day for the rest of my life.

Mr. Jenkins brought plates of food and set them on the table. "Mrs. Jenkins made a pan of fried potatoes, so she put some on your plates."

"Thank you," Callie said as the savory aroma of fried onions wafted up from the potatoes. "That was very kind."

Clayton grunted and nodded his own thanks before digging into the food on his plate. Callie bit into a piece of crisp bacon and savored the smoky flavor in her mouth.

"That is so good," she sighed and closed her eyes as she chewed.

"How long has it been since you had bacon?" Clayton asked as he shoveled up potatoes with his fork. "You act as though it were manna from heaven."

"Let's see," Callie said and rolled her eyes up in contemplation. "It's October now, and Evan dumped me at the Ellsworth back in June, so it's been about four months since I tasted bacon."

"That's too damned long to go without bacon," Clayton whistled and took a swallow of his coffee.

Callie slathered some apple butter on her biscuit. "It most certainly is." She took a bite followed by a sip of coffee. "So, what are the plans for today?"

Clayton cleared his throat. "Well, I thought I'd take you out and show you my new place."

Callie's eyes went wide. "Your new place?"

"Yah, I came across it a few weeks back," he said and swallowed some more coffee. "It needs a little fixin' up, but it will suffice for the winter."

"You're planning to stay in Kansas then?" Callie asked uneasily.

"Thinkin' on it," he said and took another bite.

He can certainly be a man of few words. It's a bit exasperating at times.

"Giving up on cowboying?" she asked and gazed out the window where people were going about their business up and down the boardwalk on both sides of dusty Front Street.

"Getting' too old for it." He followed her gaze and saw two young cowboys stumbling out of The Curly Buffalo.

"It's a life for younger men, I suppose," Callie said, and she studied the lines at the corners of his eyes, untanned from squinting into the sun. His full, silver mustache covered any lines around his mouth.

I think he's older than me, but his life on the range has kept him fit. His body is in better shape than most men our age. He's certainly trimmer around the middle than Evan. Is it even proper to wonder if he has anything else nicer than Evan's?

Callie grinned to herself as she finished her breakfast, staring at the handsome cowboy.

CHAPTER 14
A RIDE IN THE COUNTRY

Callie enjoyed the warm sun on her face and the cool breeze as they traveled southwest of Ellsworth on bumpy lanes, not much more than cattle trails.

"It's a lovely day for a ride," she said as she inhaled the scents of autumn—damp earth, fallen leaves, and new-mown fields. "How much farther is it?"

Clayton eased the buggy through a fast-moving stream and pointed to a hill on their right. "Just up there."

Callie gazed across an open field of swaying, russet ryegrass. "It's lovely," she sighed with her hand at her bosom. "What a perfect picture it makes."

"You really think so?" he asked with a grin beneath his neatly trimmed silver mustache.

"I do. However did you find this place? It's so out of the way from town."

Clayton went on to tell her about him and Dolly camping by the stream and then seeing the empty house and barn, the fenced graves, and the note on the pillow.

Callie sat with gloved fingers over her quivering

lips and tears stinging her eyes. "Oh, how sad," she whispered. "That poor man."

"Yah, I suppose so," Clayton said and took a deep breath. "I took his note to the courthouse and thought they might give me trouble over it," he said and shrugged his wide shoulders, "but they just charged me a two-dollar transfer fee and three-dollars for the delinquent taxes." He smiled as he brought the buggy to a halt in front of the house. "It's all mine now to do with as I see fit."

"And what's that going to be?" Callie asked as he helped her down. "The house could do with a coat of paint."

Typical woman; already makin' changes and she hasn't even walked in the door.

Clayton gazed into her eyes. "I'm putting some ideas together, but," he grinned down at her, "I'm gonna have to work on things a little more."

"Well, let me have a look," she said and stepped up onto the porch. "I already love it," she said, pointing to the empty swing. "All it needs is a cushion."

Clayton opened the door. "It needs a lot more than that." He motioned for her. "Come on in and have a look."

Callie followed him into the large parlor, empty except for a settee, footstool, and table. "This is nice," she said, gazing around the room as she followed him into the kitchen. She ran her hand over the finely sanded pine counters. "This is even nicer," she sighed. "Plenty of workspace in here. A woman could can up a whole garden in this kitchen."

"And store it all in here," Clayton said and opened a door to expose empty shelves, lining a huge pantry. Empty jars and lids had been left behind by the former resident along with a tall enameled pot and lid.

"Oh, my," Callie gasped as she stepped over to peer inside. "This is a space designed by a woman, that's for certain. Everything is very handily laid out." She poked her head around the corner into the washing room and door leading out onto a porch. She peeked out the window in the door and saw the area enclosing the two graves. "Do you think that was her?"

Clayton put his hands on Callie's shoulders and pulled her away from the window. "I think it probably was," he whispered into her hair and felt her tremble.

"He must have loved her very much," Callie said as she walked around the spacious kitchen. "Most men wouldn't take a woman's ideas on building into consideration."

"I don't know about that," Clayton scoffed. "I think I'd want my woman happy in her workspace."

Callie rolled her eyes. "I'm sure you would," she said with a chuckle and took his work-weathered hand. "Let's go see the bedrooms. We women work in there too, you know."

Oh, my lord. Was that an offer of her affections? She's a bold woman, but then most whores are.

Clayton led her to the child's room first where Callie brushed a hand over the ornately carved cradle and peeked into the wardrobe. "It's all just so very sad," she said as she closed the door to hide the abandoned infant garments. "I know the pain of losing a child."

"And a spouse," he said then quickly added when he saw her face darken, "in a way of sayin'."

Callie grinned at his discomfort. "Yes, in a way, I do." She took Clayton's hand again. "These walls could do with a fresh coat of whitewash, but it appears to be very well built. I don't feel any drafts around the windows."

"No," Clayton said proudly as he tugged her out of the bedroom and into the parlor where he tossed another log onto the fire, "I think Mr. Coventry was an experienced builder from back east."

"No leaks in the roof?" Callie asked as she gazed up through the exposed rafters where a few cobwebs swayed.

"Not that I've noticed," he said, "but it hasn't rained since I moved in."

"Oh," Callie gasped as he suddenly pulled her close and kissed her lips. She relaxed in his arms and surrendered to the kiss.

"Want to see the other bedroom?" he whispered breathlessly between kisses and gently pulled her to the doorway of the room she hadn't seen yet.

She followed him and her eyes went wide when she saw the neatly made bed in the room.

Is this really what I want? No respectable woman would be alone with a man in his house and especially not in his bedroom. Do I want to couple with a whore in my bed?

He saw her eyes go to the bed. "He left it here along with all her clothes," Clayton said and opened the wardrobe door to show Callie several dresses and petticoats hanging from wooden hangers.

"How sad," Callie whispered. "He must have been heartbroken over losing her and the new baby."

"I don't know that I could have just left them and all their things behind," Clayton said sadly. "I'd have wanted to have something to remember them by, I think."

"You said he had another son?" Callie asked as she pushed aside the lace curtains to peek outside. She saw a hedgerow of wild roses, the tiny leaves turning gold with the low autumn and cooler weather. "He is probably all the reminder he needs. I'm sure he sees their faces in the child's every time he looks at him."

"You're probably right," Clayton said and pulled her close again. "Does it make you uncomfortable being in my bedroom with me?" he asked suddenly.

Callie glanced at the bed again. "I suppose it should," she said with a hard swallow.

It would if you were a proper woman and not a whore.

"But it doesn't?" Clayton kissed her again and ran his hands up and down her firm, warm body.

I've never been with a whore. What am I supposed to do now?

Clayton pulled the pins from her hair and her chestnut curls came cascading down around her shoulders.

I think I'll let her take the lead here and just enjoy the ride.

He tucked a curl behind her ear then began nibbling on it, causing shivers to run through Callie's body. She moaned as his hand went to her bosom and squeezed. Callie raised her hand and began unbuttoning her dress. Not in the taunting manner she had with Caine, but casually. Callie didn't think he'd even noticed until his hand encountered her open camisole and moved eagerly to find a hard nipple.

Clayton gazed into her eyes and when she smiled, he bent to take the hard, pink mound into his mouth. Callie moaned with delight and did not resist when he removed her dress and camisole, untied the ribbon holding up her petticoat and yanked it down.

Callie kicked off her slippers and Clayton gazed at her naked body with his eyes wide. "Damn, you're one beautiful woman."

"Thank you," she replied nervously and took a seat on the edge of the bed. Callie reached for him and unbuckled his belt as he unbuttoned his shirt. He groaned as she unbuttoned his trousers and opened them to release his throbbing erection.

Damn, she sure seems to know what she's doing. What the hell am I supposed to do now? Should I ask her about the money before we go any farther?

Unsure of herself, Callie did what Evan had always liked. She bent and kissed the purple head of Clayton's erection. She felt his body tense and heard him moan as she put her lips around it and worked her tongue the way Evan had always liked. Soon he had his fingers twined in her hair and was pushing and pulling her head over the pulsing organ.

"Wait a minute," Clayton said and pushed her back onto the bed. "I don't want to waste it that way." He stared down into her face as he used one of his rough hands to push her legs apart. "Damn," he sighed as he stared at the hair covered crevasse between her smooth, creamy thighs.

Callie shivered as his hand ran up and down her inner thighs before playing in the hair for a few minutes and then probing her throbbing center. She moaned and arched up into his finger as he ran it in and out over the throbbing button of nerves. "You're wet," he sighed and stared down at her with a confused furrow in his forehead.

"I guess you're ready," he breathed, straddled her, and positioned himself to push into her.

I hope she's ready for me. I can't hold it in much longer. Do whores get pleasure from coupling the way men do? I've always wondered about that.

Clayton's fingers found her nipples and he pinched them between his thumbs and forefingers as he thrust into her repeatedly. Callie met every thrust with one of her own and clawed at his shoulders as the waves of pleasure throbbed from between her legs and sent her heart pounding. He pinched her nipples harder and an explosion of pure pleasure took her.

"Oh, my god," she screamed and arched her back up into him.

"Damned right," he groaned in return and pushed deep into her with his release. "Damn," he said again, smiled, and fell atop her, panting. "Damn," he whispered into the crook of her neck as his flaccid member slipped out of her.

Well, she certainly seemed to enjoy it, but I suppose a practiced whore is a good actress.

Clayton rolled off her onto his back and threw his arm up to wipe sweat from his brow. "Damn," he said again. "You do know how to make a fella feel good." He rolled and raised up onto his elbow to stare down at her.

Callie smiled back, enjoying the after-effects of a fulfilling coupling. The first one she'd ever truly enjoyed.

"You must have fellas lined up to have a turn with ya over at the Ellsworth."

Callie's smile vanished. She rolled off the bed and began gathering up her clothes.

Now, what's that all about?

"Hey," he gasped and reached for her. "I've got more where that came from."

Callie fought tears from streaming from her eyes. "Yah, but it's getting late and I should be getting back," she snapped and held out her hand palm up. "That'll be a dollar."

Clayton lost his grin as he stared at her upturned palm. "I knew you were a whore," he snapped and reached off the bed for his trousers. "I heard men in the saloon talking about you, Callie. They were right. You are a good poke." He dug into his pocket and brought out a shiny silver dollar. He slapped it onto her palm. "I'd almost talked myself into believing otherwise," he hissed, "but no school ma'am puts a cock in her mouth and works it the way you do."

Callie turned her back away from him as she put her clothes back on. The silver dollar burned her hand and she dropped it into the pocket of her dress as soon as she had it pulled up over her shoulders.

What a bitch.

"That fella said you liked having your nipples pinched," Clayton continued, "and you sure as hell do. He said your cunny got juicy and it sure as hell does." He struggled to talk and shove his long legs back into his denim trousers. "He said you were an experienced whore and you sure as hell seem to be." He glared at Callie as he buckled his belt.

"I'll meet you in the buggy," Callie said coolly, wrapped her shawl around her shoulders, and stomped out of the room.

Maybe I should have offered to pay more if she'd stay longer. Does a man pay by the poke or by the hour?

CHAPTER 15
AN UNEXPECTED GUEST

Sleep eluded Clayton all night. Every time he closed his eyes, he saw Callie's angry ones glaring back at him. She hadn't spoken a word to him all the way back to town. He'd practiced asking Callie to marry him all the way into town that morning. Had she not proven to be the whore he'd suspected all along, he'd probably have asked.

Why am I losing sleep over a damned whore? I thought I shed that nonsense forty years ago when I walked away from Fredericksburg and her. Thank God, I got clear on this one and didn't make a fool mistake that would tie me to another one for the rest of my life.

Twice, Clayton's mind had returned to her in his bed and he'd had to use his hand to relieve himself of a stiff, throbbing cock. Now he'd have to launder his sheets, though.

Damnable woman.

The sun shining on his face filtered through lace woke him. Clayton rolled out of bed, trudged into the kitchen, and made a pot of coffee. He brought the pot along with his tin cup into the parlor and dropped onto the settee. He filled his cup then used a piece of split wood to jab at the ashes in the fireplace.

He found some red coals and added some kindling until it caught into a flame and added a few small sticks. When they caught, Clayton laid in some larger pieces to take the early morning chill out of the room.

During the night, he'd decided to go hunting the next day. The small building between the outhouse and the barn had turned out to be a smokehouse. Some smoked meat for the winter months would be a good thing to have on hand. Clayton didn't think he'd like hunting when snow was a foot or more deep.

He dressed in a flannel shirt, loaded his rifle, put some extra cartridges in his pocket, and went out to saddle Dolly.

"I'm not gonna leave you all alone again today, girl," Clayton said and patted the horse on the neck. "You're the only girl I need, aren't you?"

He holstered the rifle and climbed into the saddle. His behind felt good in the leather. It had been his home for forty years. He glanced back at the house from the barnyard and frowned.

Maybe this whole retirement thing was a bad idea after all.

The crack of a rifle caused him to flinch and brought Clayton back to the here and now. The sound had come from across the valley in the direction of the creek. He turned the horse in that direction.

"Come on, Dolly. It sounds like we have company."

Clayton peered off through the trees while he and Dolly skirted the edge of the pasture. As he rode closer, Clayton caught the scent of wood burning and studied the tree line until he saw a thin wisp of white smoke spiraling up toward the blue autumn sky.

He slid off Dolly, took his rifle from the leather sleeve, and stepped lightly through the dry grass and across the shallow creek. A lone man sat crouched beside a low fire.

"Hey, there, mister," Clayton called, "this here's private property. It's impolite to go poachin' another man's winter game."

A mule hee-hawed loudly as Clayton stepped out of the brush growing beside the creek. The man's head jerked up, knocking his hat off, and Clayton saw a balding gray head he recognized.

"Hawk," Clayton called, "is that you?"

"Yah, 'tis me," the old man said as he fumbled for his ragged felt hat. "I didn't know this here was private property, mister." He squinted and held up a fat rabbit by the hind legs. "You're welcome ta the hare I shot. I'll just clean up my fire and me an' my mule, Bessie will be on our way."

Clayton walked closer to the old man. "Nonsense," Clayton said as he neared the fire. "Keep your rabbit. I'm sure there are plenty more here about." He held up his rifle. "I was just going out to see if I could scare up a deer or two for my smoke house."

"Smoked deer sausage is fine eats," the old man said as he stared at Clayton. "You're that young fella from Fredericksburg, ain't ya?"

"That's me, Clayton Swift." He smiled at the old man who wore dirty, fringed Indian leathers. "What are you doing up here in Kansas? When I saw you last, you were down in the Nations."

Hawk gave him a broad toothy grin. "Well, ya see," he said, "I have me an ol' injun gal down there who don't mind sharin' 'er blankets with an ol' white man from time ta time." He winked at Clayton mischievously. "I spent a season with 'er, but I'm an ol' wanderer and thought I'd wander up here to Kansas for a spell." He took a deep breath and began to cough. "Our talk got me ta thinkin' on Lil and I thought I'd head to Dodge and look 'er up." He began to cough again.

"Are you all right?" Clayton asked and rushed to his side when Hawk dropped to the ground to sit.

"These cold nights," he said and waved Clayton away. "I'll be fine once I'm up and movin' 'round a bit." Hawk poured some coffee into a blue enameled tin cup, tipped it up and swallowed. "I fear this gettin' old is a younger man's game," he said and grinned. "What are you doin' up here, boy? Guardin' private property for some rich rancher? I thought you wintered down in Texas."

"Nope," he said proudly, "guarding my own property now."

"Ya don't say," Hawk said, wide-eyed. "This here ranch is yourn? I thought ya was a cow-hand."

"Like you said," Clayton sighed with a smile, "it's a younger man's game. I thought I'd start my own little ranch and hire cowboys to run the animals while I sit warmin' my old bones by the fire."

"You need a woman to warm other things," Hawk said with a wink. "You got one of them yet?"

"One thing at a time," Clayton said with a sad smile. "One thing at a time."

"I s'pose you're right on that 'count," the old man said with a shake of his gray head. "I can only put up with a woman a few months at a time then me an' my mule gotta hit the trail again." He coughed some more.

"Why don't we clear this camp and you and the mule can come up and bunk at my place for a bit. I have a spare room, a fenced pasture, and a sturdy barn."

"You got bacon?" Hawk asked with narrowed eyes.

"Bacon, eggs, flour, and soda for biscuits, and coffee," Clayton assured him. "I don't have a bathtub yet," he sighed, "but I have a wash pan and soap."

"Who needs a wash pan an' soap?" Hawk snapped. "You ain't plannin' ta haul me off ta church, are ya?"

"No, I thought you might like to clean up a little before sleeping in a clean bed."

Hawk began clearing his camp. "Maybe you don't need no woman," he muttered. "You sorta sound like one with all your damned talk about soap an' baths an' such."

Clayton smiled and helped the old man gather his things and saddle his mule. They crossed the creek and rode through the field back to Clayton's barn. He unsaddled Dolly as well as the mule and stowed them in the barn.

"This here's a nice barn ya got here, Clayton," Hawk said as he inspected the stalls. "An ol' man could winter over good in a place like this."

"You don't have to sleep in the barn, Hawk. There's a perfectly good room in the house with a bed. It's not much more than a cot," Clayton said, "but it will be warm and dry."

"Are you sure?" the old man asked. "I can be a might troublesome."

Clayton slapped Hawk on the back. "You come bearing a fat, juicy rabbit, don't you?"

"That I do," Hawk said with a wide grin and lifted the rabbit from his bag.

"Then, come and see your room," Clayton said and motioned for Hawk to follow him to the house.

The old man shuffled after Clayton but stopped at the little picketed area and bowed his head. Clayton saw Hawk's lips moving in a muttered prayer. The old man crossed himself and glanced up at Clayton.

"I was schooled by the Jesuits after my mama passed," he said in hurried explanation. "Mama taught us our numbers and letters, but the Jesuits had a school near St. Louis, and she sent me an' my brothers there. Schoolin' weren't for me, but I think one of my brothers took the cloth. It woulda made my mama happy ta know it." Hawk took a deep breath. "I didn't stay long. I weren't much of one for all their rules an' sing-song prayers all night, so I took off an' started my wanderin' ways."

Clayton looked at the old man with new eyes. He knew about the Jesuit schools. Only educated men came out of them. If Hawk went to a Jesuit school, then he must be more than he seems.

"My mother made sure I got an education too," Clayton said. "I got six years before I started cowboyin', but it was enough to learn to read, write, and do ciphers."

"Even a cowboy needs to know how ta count them cows," Hawk said with a chuckle.

Clayton rolled his eyes. "Or subtract, when there are rustlers to contend with, marauding Indians, or flood waters."

"Indeed, indeed," Hawk said with a nod. "You're a good man, Clayton Swift and I'm proud ta know ya." He extended his feeble hand and Clayton took it.

"I'm proud to know you too, Hawk," Clayton said with a smile. "Now come on in and bring that rabbit with you so we can clean it for our Sunday supper."

"Sunday supper," Hawk sighed. "I don't think I've had a proper Sunday supper in decades." He got a far-off look in his old eyes. "Lil made me Sunday suppers once upon a time. Her boy had gone an' she was pinin' his loss. I spent some time with 'er then an' she made me fried chicken, mashed potatoes, an' cream gravy with the best biscuits I think I've ever put in my mouth." He stepped inside the warm house. "That woman could fuck," he said with a grin and a wink, "but she could surely cook too."

Clayton's face burned for a moment. "So, what do you think of the place?" he asked hurriedly as he led Hawk toward the bedroom.

Hawk shuffled through the kitchen and his eyes rested on the dirty window with cobwebs in the corners of the sills. "It could surely use a woman's touch," he mumbled as he followed behind Clayton.

CHAPTER 16
MEN!

It had been six weeks since Clayton had dropped her in front of the Ellsworth House and driven off without so much as a good-bye. He hadn't written or come by since, though Callie hadn't expected him to after their silent ride back into town.

I suppose I shouldn't have allowed what happened in his bedroom to have happened. He had to think I was a disrespectable woman.

Callie had wept over it, pondered it for hours on end, and discussed it with Lil, who'd become somewhat of a confidant over the weeks.

"Sugar," Lil had said and patted her lovingly on the knee as they sat in Callie's room sipping coffee and nibbling on a pastry, "you did absolutely nothing to make that man think you were a woman in the trade."

"I live in a whore house," Callie had wept, "and I … I let him …"

"So, you enjoyed a pleasurable afternoon in his bed," Lil said, shrugging her shoulders. "What of it? Do you think less of him because of it?" Lil took a sip of her coffee. "Of course, you don't. It's fine for a man to enjoy sex outside marriage, but if a woman does, she's accused of being a damned whore."

"He said that I must be because I put his penis in my mouth. He said only a whore could suck cock like that." Callie dabbed at her eyes with her linen kerchief.

Lil raised a gray eyebrow and grinned over her cup. "He did, did he?" She rolled her eyes. "Men are such damned hypocrites." She pulled a bit of pastry off and put it to her lips. "They want their woman to do things they enjoy," she hissed, "but call her a whore when she does them well."

"I certainly don't understand it," Callie wept.

"Don't fret over it none, sugar," Lil had sighed. "He'll either think on it and decide he's made a God-awful mistake; in which case, he'll come crawling back, begging your forgiveness, or," she said and patted Callie's knee again, "he won't and you're probably the better for it."

Callie considered Lil's words, wiped her eyes, and resolved not to shed one more tear over Clayton Swift and his pig-headed attitudes about women.

He hadn't come to her begging forgiveness, and Callie had to come to terms with it.

Maybe I'm just too old for this romance nonsense. I'm doing all right making clothes and mending. I have friends here ... better friends than I ever had before, I think.

Today Callie sat in Lil's room on a wingback settee they'd found in the basement. The green bro-cade had been horribly stained, but they'd scrubbed it with some sweet-scented soap and gotten out most of the stain. Later, Callie had recovered the settee with some new bright yellow brocade fabric, tacked down with pretty brass studs.

"I love this pretty yellow you've painted the room, Lil. It really brightens it up in here."

"Now," Lil sighed, "all I need, are those new curtains and bed things we talked about."

"Absolutely," Callie said enthusiastically. "I think Martins has some new fabric in from St. Louis. It will probably be the last he gets in before spring."

Lil pushed to her feet and reached for her cane. "Let's get to it, then."

"I'll meet you downstairs," Callie said. "I need to get my gloves and shawl from my room." She hurried out into the hall and down the stairs while Lil put herself together.

"Where are you rushing off to?" Caine asked Callie, blocking her way with his big arms at the bottom of the stairs.

"I need to get to my room," she said and tried to duck beneath his sweat-stained sleeve.

"Why don't you invite me along and let me between those pretty legs?" He grabbed Callie's shoulder with one hand and clamped her behind with the other. "I'll be in and out in no time at all," he said with a raised brow and gave her ass a hard squeeze.

"I'm sure you would," Callie sneered, "but I prefer a man who wants to take his time." She broke away and slipped beneath his arm. Callie rushed into her room and locked the door.

I can't believe that man. Why won't he just give it up? Does he really think I'm going to let him into my bed?

Callie slipped her hands into her warmest wool gloves, put on her bonnet with a scarf that went around her neck, and wrapped her heaviest shawl over her shoulders. In the lobby, Lil waited, similarly attired against the late November cold.

"Let's get down to Martins before the snow starts to fly," Lil said and opened one of the frosted glass doors.

Outside, the cold bit into Callie's cheeks. "I think it's gonna be a long, cold winter this year," she said and rubbed her hands together. Her breath condensed in the cold air under gray, cloud-laden skies.

"We're due," Lil sighed as she stepped across an icy rut in the street. "The last two were pretty warm as I recall."

"I know," Callie agreed. "I didn't have to dig my root vegetables until almost Christmas last year." She planted her booted foot on the hard surface of Front Street. "This year, the ground's been frozen solid since late October."

Callie helped Lil up onto the boardwalk. "Thank you, sugar," the older woman said as she found her balance, leaning on her cane. "I truly don't recall getting old."

"It's one of those things that slips up on a body," Callie said with a sympathetic smile as they walked together toward the mercantile with the heels of their boots clacking on the boardwalk.

The warm air inside the mercantile was welcome after the walk in the brisk air. Callie and Lil made their way to the rear of the store, where bolts of rolled fabric stood leaning against the wall.

"Oh," Lil sighed, brushing her fingers over a white cotton printed with sprays of bright yellow daffodils.

"It will certainly look pretty with your new walls," Callie said. She shifted some bolts around and pulled out on with bright white eyelet rolled on it. "Wouldn't this make a pretty dust ruffle?"

"May I help you ladies?" Mr. Martin said as he walked up behind them.

"How much is this eyelet?" Callie asked without looking the man in the eyes. She still hadn't gotten over the man's hurtful words in The Flat Iron or her dismissal from her position at the school. She could feel him staring down his beakish nose at her.

"The twelve inch is twenty-five cents a yard and the four-inch is fifteen."

"I'll take six yards of the wide and ten of the narrow," Callie said decisively to Mr. Martin, who picked up the heavy roll to carry to his cutting table.

"And what you gonna do with that, Callie?" a male voice asked. "Make yourself some fancy new work clothes to entertain in at The Ellsworth?"

Callie turned to see Evan standing in the aisle with a pretty young woman on his arm. They both chuckled as Callie's cheeks reddened.

"I see it didn't take you long to replace Polly, Evan," Callie sneered.

"I have no idea what you're talking about," Evan snapped.

"Are you going to set this one aside when she gets with child like you did poor Polly?" Callie continued. "You're a misogynistic bastard."

Evan turned to his brown-eyed companion and grinned. "Callie likes to try and show people up by using big words she thinks they won't understand." The young woman grinned at Callie. "I'm Tara Green and I've just been hired to fill the vacant position at the school."

"Evan is fond of schoolteachers," Callie said. "He used to be married to one, then he was sleeping with a girl who thought she had the job until he got her with child and refused to marry her." Callie heard Mr. Martin clear his throat loudly. "Oh," Callie added with a sly grin at the shopkeeper, "make certain you read that morality clause in your employment contract. They're real sticklers for morality here in Ellsworth."

"How many yards will I need of this," Lil asked

with a grin tugging at the corners of her rouged mouth, for a coverlet, pillow slips, and curtains?" She turned to a fidgeting Martin and said, "I'll have whatever Callie says I need and the same eyelet as her order." She picked up the fabric Mr. Martin had folded for Callie. "I'll be waiting for you up front, sugar."

"Four yards should do it along with two yards of quilt batting and two yards of plain muslin," Callie told the nervous shopkeeper.

"Yes, ma'am," Mr. Martin said and began cutting fabric, "I'll bring it up front in a minute."

Callie began to walk toward the counter when Evan grabbed her by the arm. "You don't have to be such a sour bitch, Callie."

"And you don't have to be such a philandering pig, but you are." Callie yanked her arm away and marched toward the front of the store.

He'd have just told me I sounded like a whore if I'd called him what I wanted to call him; a fucking prick. I think I like my new vocabulary.

CHAPTER 17
THE NIGHT BEFORE
CHRISTMAS IN ELLSWORTH

With no pines readily available on the flat Kansas prairie, the women took a buggy out one crisp afternoon and found a lonely cedar in a fencerow to cut and trim in the lobby of The Ellsworth House. The flimsy branches wouldn't hold heavy ornaments, so they decorated it with shredded foil tinsel, colorful fabric bows, and paper chains.

"Isn't it pretty," Mae gushed as they stood back, admiring their work. "Do you think Father Christmas will visit a whore house, Callie?"

Callie stared at the girl in dismay. Sometimes she found herself taken back by the girl's childish manner. "Did he come last year?" Callie asked, shrugging her shoulders.

"No," Mae replied wide-eyed, "but we've never had a tree here before."

Callie shrugged her shoulders again and smiled. "Then perhaps he will visit this year."

"You really think so?" the girl asked enthusiastically. "Oh, I hope so. I haven't had a visit from Father Christmas since my ma died."

Callie glanced at Lil who sat on the settee, rolling

her eyes with a grin on her powdered face. "I suppose we'll have to see about writing him a letter to let him know we have a tree this year," Callie said.

"We can do that at my next lesson," Mae gushed.

When she learned many of the young women living at The Ellsworth House could not read or write, Callie had begun hosting classes in her room two evenings a week, much to Caine's displeasure. He preferred having the women in his employ ignorant.

"An educated whore is nothing but trouble," he'd snapped at Callie when she'd mentioned the classes to him.

"An educated whore will know when she's being cheated," Callie had retorted. "Isn't that what you really mean?"

Caine had glared at her. "All whores need to know is how to fuck and how to suck cock. They have men like me to manage the business of it."

"Don't you think women who can carry on an educated conversation with a client would attract a better class of client—ones with more time and more money to spend?"

Caine furrowed his brow in thought. "You mean like bankers and lawyers?"

"And doctors and politicians," Callie added. "Those kinds of men prefer a woman they can have a little conversation with about current events and books. They'll tend to spend more time with her," Callie said.

"And more time means more money," Caine finally said. "Do you really think you can turn this bunch of low-rent trash into high-end cunny?" he asked incredulously.

"If they were educated, had nicer clothes, and

nicer furnishings in their rooms," Callie said, "the girls at Ellsworth House could become some of the most sought-after women in Kansas, commanding a much higher price for their time." Callie walked away, leaving Caine to ponder what she'd just said.

The following week, he told her to set up her classes and had given her two dollars to purchase supplies from Martin's.

"Once they can all read, we'll talk about getting them fancier clothes," Caine had snarled grudgingly.

Callie had already been making a few things in her spare time to give as Christmas gifts. When she'd seen a bolt of blush-pink China silk in the mercantile, Callie had purchased the entire ten-yard roll at fifty-cents per yard. It was a huge sum for her, but she knew her friends would be delighted with the camisoles and bloomers she planned to make from it. Three yards of quilted green velvet would become new, warm dressing gowns for Lil and Mae.

Lil's new coverlet, frilly pillow slips, curtains, and dust ruffle had brightened the woman's room so much, others in The Ellsworth House wanted the same for their rooms and paid Callie in advance for her work. Callie had not worried about money for several months and had briefly thought about finding other lodgings.

Why bother? My room is comfortable, and these women are my friends.

"You should think about opening a shop," Lil told her one afternoon as they strolled down the boardwalk to the mercantile. That Jewish tailor's shop on the other side of the bakery is empty. I heard he's moved on to Denver where there's more call for men's suits than here in Ellsworth."

"Are you serious?" Callie asked with a furrowed brow.

"Yep," Lil said, shaking her head, "I have no idea why a tailor of men's fancy clothes would have set up shop here in Ellsworth in the first place."

"No," Callie said, stopping the older woman in mid-step, "I mean about me opening a real shop. Do you really think my sewing is good enough for that?"

"Sugar," Lil said and began walking again, "you do the best work I've seen in a long, damned time, and you've got no space in your room for a cutting table. In a shop, you could spread out and maybe even get one of those new sewing machines I've seen advertisements for in the periodicals."

"Oh, my," Callie sighed, "more room would surely be nice." She took a deep breath. "But do you think I could make a go of it?"

"Sugar, you're so busy now, you seldom take time to eat anymore."

Keeping busy kept Callie's mind off Clayton and her disappointment over what had happened between them. She hadn't seen him in town and wondered if he had remained at the little farm or moved on. Mae said cowboys were a wandering breed of man and seldom settled in one place for very long.

On a whim, Callie had purchased three yards of blue flannel the same color as Clayton's eyes. She thought she would make him a shirt for Christmas, but the fabric remained folded at the bottom of her wardrobe. She couldn't see her way to taking it to him.

It would be her first Christmas as a single woman and Callie wasn't looking forward to it. She glanced at the stack of tissue-wrapped packages in her wardrobe and smiled.

At least Father Christmas will be making a stop at The Ellsworth House this year.

Snow fell heavily three days before Christmas,

bringing business at the Ellsworth House to a virtual standstill. Farmers and ranchers were too busy with their stock to come into town and townsfolk were too busy with preparations for Christmas.

Women sat in the lobby wrapped in warm dressing gowns and wool stockings against the chill, rather than their flimsy work clothes.

"I'm so bored," Trudy whined. "Let's do something."

"Like what?" Mae asked with a yawn.

"What do you think Mrs. Jenkins has at the Flat Iron tonight?" Trudy asked, staring at the other women slumped on the couches.

"Fried chicken, I think," Tabby chimed in with a grin. "Her fried chicken is the best."

Trudy stood and glared over at Caine. "Let's get dressed and go have supper, then. It's Christmas Eve after all."

Caine simply rolled his eyes, knowing there would be no business anyhow and waved them off.

"I'll get Callie," Mae said and jumped to her feet. She ran to Callie's door and knocked. "We're all going to the Flat Iron for fried chicken, Callie," Mae called through the door. "Get dressed and come with us."

Callie pulled her curtain aside and stared out at the falling snow.

As nice as hot fried chicken sounds, I'm not walking out in that mess tonight. I still have things to do to get ready for Father Christmas's visit.

She went to the door and caught Mae in the hall. "I think I'll pass, Mae," she told the girl. "But here's two-bits if you'd bring me back a plate." She held the coin out toward the pouting redhead.

"You're no fun, Callie," Mae whined as she took the coin from Callie.

"You probably just want to get me outside so you, Trudy, and Tabby can throw snowballs at me."

Mae gave her an impish grin and stuck out her tongue. "How'd you know?"

"I was your age once, you know." Callie grinned before returning to her room. She had a few finishing touches to add to a pair of bloomers and wanted to get the set wrapped to add to the pile in her wardrobe.

The quiet in The Ellsworth without the girls chattering in the lobby and the dampening of the outside sounds by the falling snow was disconcerting. Callie tied the ribbon on the package and added it to the others when her door opened.

She turned to see Caine creeping into her room. "I don't recall inviting you in," Callie said as she closed the wardrobe.

I don't want the bastard ruining my surprise.

He took a tentative step toward her. "I think I want to take you up on your offer now, Callie," he said and began fumbling with his belt buckle.

"What offer?" Callie asked nervously.

"The one you made in here that day you took off your clothes." He licked his lips. "I think I'll have it now," he said and in one quick movement, he had his belt off in one hand and yanked at Callie's dressing gown with the other.

"Get your hands off me and get out of my room," Callie shouted but stood still as he pulled off her dressing gown and threw it to the floor.

I refuse to give him the fight he wants.

"No," he spat back at her and pulled at the yoke of her nightdress. "I'll have what's mine now. You owe me twenty-dollars." He tugged hard and the tiny buttons flew to the floor.

Damnit, I hate sewing on those tiny buttons.

Callie struggled a bit as Caine used his bulk against her. She groaned mentally when she heard the cotton fabric of her nightdress rip as he tore it from her trembling body. There would be no bluffing her way out of this and if she screamed, there were no girls left in the lobby to hear her.

"Evan said I should show you who's boss around here," he said as he pushed her face down onto the bed. "I've been studying a while on how to do that and decided to do what my daddy did to show us kids who was boss at home."

Is Evan the one I have to thank for this? I bet he's been goading the big bastard all along.

Callie couldn't see Caine draw his arm back holding the belt, but she screamed in pain as it came down across the tender flesh of her bare backside.

She tried to squirm away with every stinging lash but refused to beg Caine to stop. It was bad enough that she couldn't control her tears. Her refusal to beg infuriated Caine and brought the strap down across her behind, back, and legs for what seemed like an eternity.

"Are you ready to give me what I want now, Callie?" Caine growled and rolled Callie onto her stinging back. He leered down at her and the scar on his cheek puckered grotesquely. He began running his hands over her bosoms, stopping to twist her nipples when he came to them.

"Are you ready?" he yelled and grabbed a hand full of her hair. He pulled and shook her head. "Yah," Caine said, grinning lasciviously down at her, "I think you're ready now."

Callie didn't know when he'd taken off his pants, but he climbed onto the bed, straddling her and began to crawl over her shivering body with his erect cock leading the way.

What a disgusting pig.

"Evan says you can do wondrous things to a cock with your mouth, Callie, and I want to see if that's true." He scooted forward until the oozing purple head pushed against her trembling lips. He yanked more hair. "Open up, bitch," he hissed as he pressed harder into her mouth, "and if you even think about biting me," he gave her hair another vicious yank, "I'll use my fists like Evan told me to."

When I get out of this, I'm gonna kill both of you fucking bastards.

Caine forced his cock into Callie's mouth and sighed as it slid over her hot tongue. "Give it a good lick," he demanded. "Oh, yah," he sighed when she complied.

I may as well do what he says, or he'll probably kill me, but I'm not going to make it fun for him and show any fear.

Callie scraped her teeth over the delicate skin and Caine twisted his hand in her hair. "I told you not to bite." He pushed his cock in until she gagged before pulling back. "I thought you'd be able to take more than that," he hissed as he pumped into her mouth.

"Your mouth is no better than any of the other bitches around here," he growled and slapped the side of Callie's head. "Let's test the other holes."

He flopped Callie over onto her belly. "You're colored up really nice, Callie. I hope you enjoyed that little lesson." Caine chuckled. "I'll be glad to do it again the next time if you want."

She flinched when he poked a finger into one of the tender welts rising across her back. "What, no smartass mouth tonight?"

Callie could hear the smile in his taunt. She remained silent and still.

"No, well, let's see if I can get a rise out of you

with this." Callie took a deep breath when Caine's fingers began probing between her bruised ass cheeks. "Ah, there it is," he sighed as he jammed a finger into her anus. Warm liquid flowed down her ass as Caine let out a stream of spittle. "I don't wanna go in dry and I'm sure you don't have a tin of lard in here for this like the other girls." He chuckled again.

When he pushed into her, it was all Callie could do to keep from screaming with the pain. She pressed her face into the cotton coverlet and bit hard.

I'm not giving the son-of-a-bitch the satisfaction of hearing me scream. I'm not.

"Now this is as nice as I thought it would be, Callie." He chuckled as he grunted. "Evan said this was virgin territory. I can't believe he never tried it." He dug his big fingers into her already throbbing ass cheeks. "I guess it' not every man's cup of tea, but I've always liked it."

Caine shoved and grunted a few more times before pulling out. "I'm going to finish in that pretty little nest you showed me, though."

Callie was filled with so much relief to have him out of her ass that she didn't even notice when he slid down a bit and shoved his hard cock into her cunny.

"Damn, woman," he snarled, "you're as dry as a week-old biscuit." He pulled out of her and rolled Callie onto her back again.

"Maybe this will get your damned juices flowing again." He drew back his big hand and slapped her across both cheeks. "Evan said it always worked for him."

Callie saw stars for a minute and was certain she'd heard the bone crack in her jaw. With her tongue, she wiggled a tooth. Her face, so red from the slap, she was certain he wouldn't notice how red it was from anger.

You and Evan Jamison are both dead men.

CHAPTER 18
FATHER CHRISTMAS VISITS

After Caine left her room, whistling a happy tune, Callie sobbed into her pillows with pain and humiliation. She laid on her belly because her back stung and throbbed from his abuse. She didn't even have the strength or will to get up and clean up the mess he'd left between her legs.

"Here's your chick …" Mae said, skipping into Callie's room. "Callie?" she gasped and came running to the bed. "Oh, God, what the hell happened?" She set the plate of food on the vanity. "What happened to you, Callie?"

"Will you get Lil?" Callie whispered, pushing up painfully on her elbows.

"Sure, Callie," Mae said and ran from the room.

"Oh, dear God, how do I explain this?

Callie struggled to her feet, picked up her discarded dressing gown, and wrapped it around her body to cover the purple welts left by Caine's belt. She stumbled to her washbasin and poured some water into a cup. Callie cringed when she saw her bruised and swollen face in the mirror.

Evan Jamison, you are a fucking dead man.

She wet a cloth and covered her face with it. The

cool cloth felt soothing. Callie cringed and let the cloth fall back into the basin when her door opened, fearing it was Caine returning for more.

"Oh, my God, Callie," Lil gasped as she rushed to Callie's side. "Let me look at that," she whispered and took the cloth from the water.

With her fingers, Lil gently probed Callie's bruised face. She flinched when Lil's fingers pressed into a spot on her lower left jaw. "I think he's broken your jaw, sugar. Who did this to you?"

"Caine," Callie whispered. "Caine did it."

"I'm gonna kill that son-of-a-bitch," Mae hissed. "Look what he did to her back," Mae told Lil.

Callie tried to fight her, but Lil tugged the dressing gown down off her back. She heard Lil gasp when she saw Callie's back striped in purple welts.

"Oh, dear God, sugar, what did that animal do to you?" Lil turned to Mae. "Take that bowl outside and bring some of that snow. I need to put it on her jaw and on these bruises. Do any of you girls have any yarrow salve?"

Mae took the enameled wash bowel. "We all keep yarrow in our things for the randy assholes," she said, rolling her green eyes.

"Well, get me some," Lil snapped as she eased Callie onto the bed.

"Yes, ma'am," Mae said and hurried out of the room with the empty washbowl tucked under her arm.

"Let's get you comfortable, sugar," Lil whispered in the same tone a mother might use with a sick child. "Rest is the best medicine right now. I'll put some ice on the bruises to take them down and rub some yarrow on them."

The door opened and Trudy and Tabby crept

into the room. "Mae said Caine did this to her?" Trudy asked with narrowed eyes.

"He did," Lil said and brushed the hair away from Callie's sweaty face.

"Damnit," Trudy hissed, turned, and stormed out of the room.

"She's gonna fucking kill him," Tabby whistled and followed Trudy into the hall.

"Not if I get to him first," Callie mumbled before closing her eyes.

"I think you're gonna have to get in line, sugar," Lil whispered as she sponged cool water on Callie's bruised face.

☙❧

MAE SCOOPED snow into the bowl. The lantern outside the door lit the snowy street. Someone on a horse stopped in front of the Ellsworth. "It's Christmas Eve, mister," Mae said in a disgusted tone and stood. "We're not seein' customers tonight."

The man studied Mae's face. "You're Callie's friend, aren't you? You helped me pick out a shirt with her once."

Mae's eyes went wide. "You're that cowboy—the one who called her a whore." Mae put her hands on her hips, awkwardly balancing the bowl of snow.

"Yep," he sighed, "that'd be me. Is she in there?" He nodded toward the Ellsworth.

"She is, but she's not seeing anyone tonight either."

"Not seeing anyone?" Clayton asked with a raised brow.

"She's ... eh ... she's ill."

"Ill?" Clayton asked in a concerned tone. "Is she going to be all right?"

"Yah," Mae said as she pushed past the tall cowboy. "She'll be fine." She turned back to the man. "You really have some nerve coming here after all this time. You called Callie a whore for no good reason. I think you broke her heart you know." Mae turned back to the door. "She cried for days in her room, you, big, stupid shit." Mae went inside and slammed the door, leaving Clayton standing open-mouthed in the snow.

Well, that didn't go very well.

"I guess we have to go back home, Dolly.

The big horse huffed and pawed at the snow.

"OK, I guess we can stay at the livery until tomorrow. It's not exactly what I planned for our Christmas though."

What did I have planned? Did I honestly think she was gonna just fall into my arms?

❧

CALLIE WOKE and saw Lil sleeping in the chair. "Lil?" Callie whispered.

Lil got to her feet and shuffled to sit on the edge of the bed. "How are you feeling, sugar?" She brushed hair out of Callie's face.

Callie groaned as she tried to roll over. "I think I'll live."

"I don't know about Caine, though," Lil said with a soft chuckle. "Trudy went after him with a butcher knife. Mae said she chased him out into the snow and then came back in with blood on the knife and locked all the doors behind her."

"What time is it?" Callie asked, bolting up in the bed.

"Hush, sugar," Lil said and pushed Callie back down by her shoulders.

"Is it Christmas?"

Lil chuckled. "It has been Christmas for about four hours."

"Oh, good," Callie said with a relieved sigh, "I haven't missed it, then." She sat up, pushed the blankets aside, and groaned as she swung her legs off the bed. Callie pulled her dressing gown tight and went to the wardrobe. "I promised Mae that Father Christmas would come tonight." She carefully lifted out the stack of wrapped packages.

"What did you do?" Lil asked as Callie handed her the packages.

"I made Christmas," Callie sighed as she lifted out one final package. She would put it under the tree, although he wouldn't be here to get it. "Come on," Callie sighed, "let's put these under the tree." She moved awkwardly toward the door. "I promised Mae Father Christmas would visit The Ellsworth House this year. She sent him a letter."

Lil shook her head as she trudged behind Callie with the packages crinkling in her arms. "You're a better woman than me, Callie Jamison."

CHAPTER 19
ANOTHER YEAR COME
AN' GONE

Clayton sat comfortably before the fire, enjoying the aromas coming from the kitchen. Since his arrival, Hawk had taken up most of the domestic duties, including the cooking. Clayton had been thrilled to find the old man an exceptional cook.

"Supper will be ready in two shakes of a coon's tail," the old man called from the kitchen.

"Smells good," Clayton replied and stood. His joints throbbed from the cold weather.

Hawk was also a stickler for the niceties of living in a house and demanded they eat at the table like 'civilized' human beings when he cooked a meal.

"'Tis just ham an' black-eyed peas with some cornbread to go along," Hawk said as he set the table with china plates they'd found in a hutch. "Sit down here, now and I'll have it served up in a minute. My mama always started the New Year with black-eyed peas. Said it were for good luck in the year ta come."

Clayton grinned and sat. "Where'd you learn to cook, old man?"

Hawk brought a plate of hot cornbread to the table. "Learnt most of it from my mama," he said with a toothy grin, "but I picked up this an' that here an' there over the years." Hawk left and returned with a crock of soft butter. "Mama always tolt us boys we had ta learn ta cook for ourselves 'cause we mighten not always have a woman about ta do for us."

"Sadly," Clayton said and nodded, "I fear that's true."

Clayton busied himself with cutting the steaming yellow cake while Hawk dipped up plates of peas with junks of fatty pork floating in savory brown sauce.

"I see you're wearin' that there shirt again," Hawk said, nodding at the blue flannel shirt he'd returned home with after his trip into town on Christmas Eve.

"It's a nice, warm shirt," Clayton said as he slathered butter on a thick square of sweet cornbread.

Hawk rolled his eyes as he set plates of peas on the table. "An' it wouldn't have nothin' ta do with that woman who made it for ya?"

"Well, maybe a little," Clayton said with an uneasy grin.

I still can't believe she made me a shirt for Christmas after I was such an ass.

Clayton's mind wandered back to standing outside the Ellsworth House on Christmas Day and waiting nervously for someone to answer after he'd knocked. The door had been locked.

The pretty young redhead had answered. "What are you doing here again, cowboy?" she'd snapped. "It's Christmas Day and we're not seeing customers today."

She'd tried to close the door, but Clayton had stopped her with his hand on the frame. "I'd like to speak to Callie, please."

The girl had turned to look back into the room where Clayton could hear women chattering and laughing. "Miss Callie ain't seein' visitors today, either." A broad smile brightened her freckled face. "Father Christmas visited last night and we're still opening our surprises, but Miss Callie is still under the weather."

"I just want to tell her Happy Christmas," Clayton had persisted.

Someone said something to the girl, and she turned away from the door. "Just wait here for a minute," she said and pushed the door shut.

When the redhead returned, she had a package wrapped in red tissue paper and tied with a bright green ribbon in her petite, freckled hand. "Here," she said and shoved the package out the door. "I can't fathom why, but Father Christmas left this here for you."

She bared her even, white teeth. "I don't think you deserve a present, though," she had snarled at him, "You were a very naughty boy to treat Miss Callie the way you did. All she did was love you and you called her a whore for it." Before slamming the door in Clayton's face, the girl had hissed, "Miss Callie ain't no damned whore. I can tell you that for certain because I'm one."

Clayton had put the package into his saddlebag and waited to open it until he was home, sitting in front of his warm fire. He untied the ribbon and unfolded the filmy colored paper. Inside was a flannel shirt. He studied it and could tell it had been sewn by a practiced hand. There was also a short note written in a neat, feminine script.

Clayton,

I don't know when or if you will ever get this, but I saw the fabric at Martins and thought it would make a fine shirt for a man working in the cold. I hope you are well, and the farming life is suiting you.

I'm very busy with orders from the girls in the house and others around town as well. Lil thinks I should open a shop here. I'm thinking on it.

Happy Christmas,
Callie

"You studyin' on that woman now?" Hawk grumbled as he crumbled some cornbread into his peas.

"I suppose I am," Clayton sighed.

Hawk shook his gray head as he shoveled peas into his mouth. "You was wrong ta treat 'er like you done, boy," Hawk scolded. "You treated 'er like filth and yet she made ya that there nice shirt," he said pointing with his fork. "That should tell ya somethin' 'bout the kind of woman she really is and how she feels 'bout ya."

"You're right, Hawk," Clayton sighed, "but what am I gonna do about it now? She won't even see me."

"Write her a letter," Hawk said. "Women like fancy words. Tell 'er you was a damned fool and want ta make it up ta her somehow."

"I wouldn't know where to begin," Clayton sighed and picked up his coffee cup.

"Just tell 'er how ya feel, boy." Hawk bit into some cornbread. "Women is all 'bout feelin's and the like."

"I suppose I could do that," Clayton said. "I should thank her for the shirt, at least."

"When a woman gives a man somethin' like that," he said and pointed to Clayton's shirt, "it's called a token. The ladies in ol' England used ta give knights tokens before they went into battle. Somethin' ta remember 'em by." Hawk reached into his breast pocket and pulled something out. He unfurled it and Clayton saw a dainty, embroidered kerchief. "Lil give this ta me a very long time ago," he said sadly as he fingered the delicate embroidery. "She said it were a token an' ta keep it close ta my heart in memory of 'er."

He handed it to Clayton, and he saw the letters LC neatly stitched onto the cloth in an ornate script. Pink flowers and greenery surrounded the elaborate letters.

"It's pretty," Clayton said as he handed the cherished token back to Hawk.

Hawk folded the kerchief and returned it to his pocket. "I've carried it right here next to my heart for nigh on forty years now," he sighed. "I'd hoped on returnin' it to 'er someday."

"Did you love her—a whore who sold her body to other men?" Clayton asked uneasily.

"Still do," the old man sighed as he patted the pocket containing the kerchief. "An' I told ya before, Lil done what she done 'cause she had no other way ta make ends meet for 'er an' that boy."

"If you say so," Clayton said and emptied his cup. "I still think she could have done other things to make ends meet like taking in washing or doing mending for folks like Callie does."

Hawk shook his head as he chewed. "You don't understand the attitudes of folks at that time 'bout the injuns. Ta them tight-assed folks in Fredericksburg, Lil had soiled 'erself beyond all reckonin' when she give herself ta them bucks that night. Nobody woulda done no business with 'er."

"Men did," Clayton retorted hotly. "Men gave her their business."

"Yah, but that were in the dark of night where nobody could see their dealin's," Hawk sighed, shaking his gray head. "Lil an' that youngin woulda starved ifn she hadn't sold 'erself like she done." Hawk shrugged his slumped shoulders. "It were all she could do an' she didn't like it none neither."

"If you say so," Clayton said as he pushed away from the table. "Thank you for another wonderful meal, Hawk. I'm gonna go out and check on the animals then I think I'll write that letter."

"Good for you, boy," Hawk said as he carried the dirty dishes into the kitchen. "Feelin's," he called, "remember that women like ta hear 'bout feelin's."

CHAPTER 20
FEELINGS

Callie sat with Clayton's letter clutched in her hands as the sunshine warmed her shoulders.

Callie,

A friend told me I should write and tell you how I feel. I fear I'm not the best at this sort of thing. Thank you for the shirt. It fits good and is warm. It was an unexpected surprise.

I am truly sorry for giving you insult the way I did. It was unforgivable, but I ask your forgiveness anyhow. First, let me say that our afternoon together was truly pleasurable. I think I will never forget it. No woman has ever given me such joy and I think fondly on it often.

Your young redheaded friend was right in telling me I had it wrong about you. She said you were not in the same business as her and the others living at The Ellsworth House. I'm of a mind to believe her and hope you can find it in your heart to forgive me for my misthoughts on the subject.

I'm a lonely old man, Callie and a foolish one. I have an unforgiving nature and that, I fear, has not served either one of us well. I hope you can find it in your heart to forgive this old fool and reply to this letter at the Ellsworth Post Office where I have rented a box.

Sincerely,

Clayton Swift

. . .

CALLIE READ THE LETTER AGAIN. She didn't know what to make of it. Someone knocked at her door and Callie refolded the letter and tucked it into the pocket of her apron before getting up to unlock her door.

Since Caine's visit, Callie kept her door securely locked and had added a sliding bolt as well. The man had returned to The Ellsworth House two days after Christmas with a new cut on his left cheek given to him by Trudy. It matched the puckered scar on his right. As it had healed, the slice drew up the other corner of Caine's mouth to give him a horrifying perpetual grin. It made Callie's skin crawl and when he caught her looking at him, Caine would take hold of his belt buckle and shake it ominously at her.

That man is never going to get close enough to touch me again.

"Who is it?" Callie called before sliding the bolt.

"It's Lil, Callie. May I come in?"

"Just a second," Callie sighed with relief and unlocked the door. "Come on in," she said and pulled open the door for Lil to enter.

"How are you doin', sugar?" Lil asked as she strolled into the room.

"I'm better," Callie told her as she relocked the door and slid the bolt into place.

"I really don't think that ass is gonna be botherin' you again, sugar, but I suppose it's better to be safe than sorry." Lil dropped into the sun-warmed chair and Callie took a seat on her bed.

"I was sorry once," Callie sighed, "and I don't intend to go through that hell again."

Lil nodded her head. "I took more than my share of beatings," she hissed. "It's all part of doing business, but what that bastard did to you was unforgivable." Lil shook her silver-gray head. "Pimps do that sort of thing to keep their women in line," she snarled, "but Caine's not your pimp. He had no right."

"He thought he did." Callie got up and poured coffee into two delicate porcelain cups. She handed one to Lil.

"Well, he didn't. I don't care what cursed dealings he had with your former husband," Lil spat before taking a sip of coffee.

Callie ran her finger over her cheek in the spot where Caine now wore a scar. "I think he knows that now," she said with a feeble grin.

Lil rolled her eyes. "I think he knows he'd best keep his hands to himself," she snarled, "and his cock in his pants, as far as you're concerned."

"I hope you're right," Callie sighed. "I hate living in fear like this."

"Have you given any more thought to opening that shop?"

"That's not going to happen, I fear," Callie said with disappointment thick in her voice.

"Why is that, do you need money for the rent?"

Callie shook her head. "No, I have enough for the rent and the deposits, but the Martins own the building with the empty tailor shop."

"So?" Lil said and took another sip of her coffee.

"So," Callie sighed, "me and my disreputable clientele are not what they want in their damned building."

"You mean the same disreputable clientele who spend their hard-earned money in their damned mercantile?"

"Exactly the same," Callie hissed.

Lil stood and walked to the stove where she

poured herself another cup of coffee. "I wish there was another place in this damned town to shop."

"It will take longer," Callie said with a grin, but I'm considering doing all my shopping by mail order from now on out. I wrote off to St. Louis for fabric samples and a catalog."

Lil's eyes went wide. "That's a good idea, sugar. I know a fella from Abilene. He and his wife sell goods from a tinker's wagon. I bet I could get them to come to town. He sells all sorts of things from that wagon and I bet he'd be willing to increase his stock if he thought there was a call for it." She winked at Callie and grinned as she sat again.

"That would put a nice thorn in Martins' side, wouldn't it?"

"It certainly would," Lil said with a chuckle. "Now we must think on what to do about getting you a shop on Front Street," Lil said with an impish grin.

"I don't think there are any other empty storefronts now," Callie said sadly.

After giving Lil's suggestion considerable thought, Callie had decided to look into renting the empty tailor's shop. She had strolled down to the building one day, peeked into the windows, and been astonished to see a large cutting table as well as several dress-forms left behind by the former occupant.

The sign in the window had said to inquire at Martins Mercantile and she had. Mrs. Martin had been less than enthusiastic about Callie's plans to open a dress shop in the building.

"And who exactly would your clientele be, Mrs. Jamison? The woman had asked haughtily.

"I've been quite busy with orders from women at The Ellsworth and others in town," Callie had said proudly.

"Those are not women I'd want to encourage in

a building of ours," Mrs. Martin had said. "I don't think we can, in good moral continence, rent our building to you, Mrs. Jamison if that's who you intend to sell to."

"Oh, I see," Callie said and left the counter to stroll about the cramped aisles. At a table near the rear of the store, Callie examined a corset and a folded stack of cotton undergarments.

I see all right. The bitch thinks I'm going to steal her damned customers away.

Callie had tossed the shabbily constructed garment back onto the table before storming past Mrs. Martin and out of the mercantile.

She's absolutely right. I fully intend to.

"How much do you think it would cost to build a small storefront building?" Callie asked Lil.

Lil sipped more coffee and stared off in contemplation. "I don't know. If you already had the lot, probably no more than two or three hundred dollars. Why?"

Callie set her cup back on the table. "Just wondering," she said. "Just wondering. Two or three hundred is a good bit more than I have, though and I don't have a lot to build on either."

"There are several of those to be had," Lil snorted.

Callie's hand brushed over her pocket and Clayton's letter.

"Have you ever been in love, Lil?" Callie asked, completely changing the subject.

Lil ran a hand over her gray hair. "I was terribly in love with my husband," Lil sighed. "He wasn't much of a husband, really. He gambled away our money and slept with other women, but I loved him. He was handsome and whisked me off my feet with tales of adventures on the wild Texas frontier," Lil said with color in her cheeks. "I was very young and very stupid."

Callie thought about Evan and sighed, "Some of us were old and stupid. Was there ever anyone else?"

Lil's lips turned up in a soft smile that reflected in her old eyes. "There was one fella back in Texas who I surely could have loved, but he was the wandering sort and would be gone for months at a time." She took a deep breath. "I had a child to think of and couldn't pin my hopes on a man like that."

Callie touched the pocket with the letter inside. "I know what you mean."

"In my line of work," Lil sighed, "developing feelings for a man is a useless endeavor. It only brings heartache and disappointment in the end."

"In my experience," Callie said, "developing feelings for any man brings nothing but disappointment and heartache."

CHAPTER 21
DISAPPOINTMENTS

Clayton tore open the letter before he was out of the Post Office. He recognized her neat script on the envelope before he saw her name. Once open, however, Clayton feared what her words might be and waited until he reached the sunny street to read Callie's reply to his letter, begging her forgiveness.

Clayton,

I'm glad the shirt fit. I made it by guestimation of your size. I'm glad you are still at your farm. It's a lovely place and suits you.
I'm glad you no longer think I'm a whore, but I find it difficult to reconcile that with the pain your words inflicted upon me. I don't understand how you could have thought that of me. I explained the circumstances of my living accommodations and don't know why you didn't believe me. I never lied to you.

I value honesty very highly. I think you are a good man, Clayton, but I think someone hurt you deeply.

*Was she a professional woman? Is that why you
harbor such deep resentment toward them?
At this point, I may be able to forgive your hurtful
words, but I don't think I can forget them as easily.
I'm sorry if that is not what you wanted to hear, but
it is truthful.*

*I too think back fondly on our afternoon together until
its end. I'm sorry to say that still pains me. I hope you
can understand that.*

*I have been very busy with my seamstress work and
hope to have my own shop in the near future. I have
been to the bank about financing, though the prospects
are dim. I fear other men in this town share your opin-
ions of me and the women here at the Ellsworth who
are my friends and my customers.
I hope you will write again and tell me about your life
on your land. spring will be here soon, and I bet it
will be beautiful there.*

*Fondly,
Callie*

CLAYTON READ the letter three times before refolding
it and stuffing it into his saddle bag. He led Dolly up
the street and looped her reins around a post in front
of the Curly Buffalo.

"What can I get ya?" the barman asked.

"Beer," Clayton said as he leaned against the bar
beside two men in suits.

"You're not going to believe what that silly wife
of Jamison's was in the bank asking for the other
day," a portly gray-headed man said with a chuckle.

"What now?" the other asked. "She was in the
store a week or so back wanting to rent my building

down on South to open a damned dress shop for her whore friends."

Clayton glanced down the bar and recognized the skinny owner of the mercantile.

"The same," the banker said with a chuckle. "Now she wants to buy a lot and build one."

"Ridiculous woman," Martin snorted. "What decent woman in Ellsworth would shop where whores shop?"

"All of 'em," Clayton said and took a sip of his beer.

"Excuse me?" Martin said in an irritated tone as he glared down the bar at Clayton.

"You sell to the whores when they come into your mercantile," Clayton said pointedly, "and all the decent women in Ellsworth still shop at your store."

"He's got a point," the banker snorted.

"That's different," Martin snapped, "mine is the only mercantile in town."

"And Mrs. Jamison's would be the only dress shop," the banker said. "Evidently she's been doing a good business out of her room at the Ellsworth House and wants to expand. She brought me a quite detailed earnings report with the breakdown of material costs and profit margins," he said with a raised brow.

"Well," Martin sneered with a raised brow, "she's working out of the Ellsworth. You know what kind of profits the women make there."

"Was her presentation professional?" Clayton asked the banker.

"What?" the banker asked, turning to Clayton.

"If a man had come in with the same business proposal," Clayton asked, "would you consider giving him the loan?"

"But she's not a goddamned man," Martin snapped. "A woman has got no place in business."

"I'll be sure to mention that to your wife the next time I'm in the mercantile," Clayton said and winked at the grinning banker. "How many whores would you say are in Ellsworth?"

The banker furrowed his brow. "Probably twenty or so living here full time and double or triple that number during the cattle season. Why?"

"You have a wife?" Clayton persisted.

The banker nodded. "And two daughters."

"And how often do they require new dresses, underthings, and frilly bits?"

The banker's eyes went wide as a smile spread across his face. "I think I see your point, Mr. Swift."

"I don't suppose *you'd* be willing to co-sign a loan for her?" Martin said.

"You own property around here?" the banker asked Clayton.

"Six-hundred-forty acres out on Clear Spring Road," Clayton said proudly.

"Jim Coventry's place?" the banker asked with a raised brow. "We went to church with him and Jane." The banker shook his head slowly. "It was a sad thing about his wife and their baby."

"I heard you just walked in there and squatted that place," Martin sneered.

"I have a transferred deed from Mr. Coventry filed at the courthouse," Clayton said. "I own it all legally."

"Humph," Martin snorted into his beer.

"Would you?" the banker said to Clayton.

"Would I what?" Clayton asked and sipped his beer.

"Be willing to put your property up as collateral for Mrs. Jamison's loan." The banker said skeptically.

"What man would risk his property on the whims of a flighty woman?" Martin jeered.

"I would," Clayton said.

"If you make that loan, Ted, Evan Jamison will have your job," Martin snarled, "He's the biggest depositor at Ellsworth Bank and Trust."

"And I work for the bank's stockholders, not Evan Jamison," the banker said to Martin. "A questionable loan backed by a six-hundred-forty-acre farm with a clear deed is a good bet for the bank any day."

"You're both fools," Martin snarled, slammed his mug down on the bar, and stormed out.

"When would you like to come in and sign the contract, Mr. Swift?"

"I have one condition," Clayton said and drained his mug.

"What condition?" the banker asked with a raised brow.

"I don't want Mrs. Jamison knowing anything about my part in this. I want her to think she's getting this loan on her own merits."

"You don't want her to know you're putting your place on the line for her? Is that wise? I've already explained to Mrs. Jamison that the bank can't really make a legal loan to a woman. A woman can't own property in her name alone. I suppose I can slip this by the stockholders, however, with your name on the loan as a co-owner of the property." The banker said, wide-eyed.

Clayton grinned. "I have complete faith in Mrs. Jamison's business acumen, Mr. Howard."

Callie is a smart woman. She wouldn't be going into this if she didn't think she could make a go of it.

CHAPTER 22
MAKING A GO OF IT

Callie sat in Ted Howard's office, shifting nervously in the hard, wooden chair.

You'd think they'd at least offer a comfortable chair to sit in when you're about to sign your life away.

"Good afternoon, Mrs. Jamison," Mr. Howard said as he took a seat behind his wide oak desk. "I hope you realize this is highly unusual and I've been put under close scrutiny by the stockholders for making this decision."

"Because I'm a woman?" Callie asked uneasily, "Or because my business will deal with disreputable women?"

Mr. Howard grinned uneasily and ran a bulbous finger around his tight collar. "A little of both, if the truth be told," he sighed, "but I make loan decisions based on the merits of the business proposal." He took a deep breath and gave Callie a nervous smile. "And after some discussions, I've had of late, I can certainly see the merits of your proposal, Mrs. Jamison. Women need clothes, and certain women," he said with a raised brow, "need them more so than others."

"I'm very happy you see it that way, Mr. Howard," Callie said with a relieved smile.

I wonder who he's been talking to. Maybe he's a regular visitor to one of the girls in town.

"Have you found a piece of property on which to build?"

"Yes," Callie said. "Mr. Caine has been persuaded to part with one of his lots adjacent to The Ellsworth."

Trudy and her butcher knife was more than gentle persuasion.

Mr. Howard raised a brow. "An excellent location."

"You have a builder in mind?"

"Jim Toliver," Callie said with a smile. "He's been highly recommended to me."

"A good man," Howard said with a nod, "and familiar with the way we handle construction loans here at the bank. Will Mr. Caine be coming to see me for his payout on the lot or have you made other arrangements?" Mr. Howard asked with an impish grin.

Not the kind of arrangement you have in your filthy mind.

"That's been taken care of," Callie said and pulled a folded piece of paper from her bag. "Here is the deed all made out to me."

"Very good," Mr. Howard said, taking the paper from Callie's hand.

"And here is my contract with Mr. Toliver for the construction of the building."

"Excellent," he said, took the paper, and studied it. "Your loan is for four hundred dollars. The lot has been taken care of and Mr. Toliver's contract is for three hundred dollars. What will the other hundred dollars be used for, if I may ask? Nothing frivolous I hope."

Callie rolled her eyes. "Fabric and notions, Mr. Howard. A seamstress needs fabric and notions."

"Of course, of course," he said, "and I suppose you'll be ordering that from Martin's?"

"Hardly," Callie huffed. "I found a wholesale supplier in St. Louis for half the price Martin asks. I'll be ordering from them. They will ship on the train. I'll need a draft from my account to send along with my order."

"Mr. Howard raised an eyebrow. "I would have thought you'd want to spend your money in our community, Mrs. Jamison."

"I'm a businesswoman, Mr. Howard and must make my decisions based on sound business practices. The Martins have made it very clear to me that they are not interested in doing business with me, therefore I am forced to take my business outside the community."

"I see," Mr. Howard mumbled. "I see." He pushed a long document in front of Callie. "Here is your contract, Mrs. Jamison. You can see here that your loan is made at an annual percentage rate of five percent and …"

"And that's about two and a half percent higher than any of your other loans of record," Callie said snidely as she studied the neatly printed paragraphs on the page.

"This is considered a high-risk loan, Mrs. Jamison, thus the higher rate of interest," he said uneasily.

"Of course," Callie sighed.

"Your monthly payment will be nine dollars for ten years," he continued for a total payout to the bank of one thousand and eighty dollars at the end of the loan period."

"And if I want to pay it off early to save on that ungodly interest?"

"Any amount you pay over your regular monthly payment would go toward the principle, Mrs. Jamison, and would pay down the loan amount quicker." Mr. Howard smiled, took a deep breath, and continued. "You are more than welcome to do just that. I will supply you with an amortization schedule that you should mark off every month when you make a payment, so you know what your payoff amount is at any given time."

As Callie took the pen in hand to sign the contract, the office door burst open and Carl Martin came storming in, face red with rage.

"I've had about enough of this bitch, Ted," Martin bellowed, wide-eyed as he slammed the door.

"Excuse me," Callie gasped.

"What is going on, Carl," Mr. Howard said as he stood to face the fuming mercantile owner. "You're interrupting a business meeting."

"I was just down having a drink at the Curly Buffalo, and Jim Toliver told me that this tight-assed cunny here has ordered him to buy his building supplies from the mill in Abilene."

"Is that true, Mrs. Jamison?" Howard asked sternly.

Callie put a hand to her bosom. "I didn't tell him to buy the supplies in Abilene," she said, defiantly glaring at Mr. Martin. "I just told him to buy them anyplace, but Martin's."

"She can't do that," Martin seethed at the banker. "We've always had a gentleman's agreement with the bank that the materials for any construction project in Ellsworth would be purchased from my mercantile."

"Well, there you are," Callie said and defiantly

shrugged her shoulders, "I'm no gentleman. There's no implied agreement with me."

"That's it," Martin yelled, "You'll be making no fabric orders through my store for your whores' garb."

Callie smiled at Mr. Howard, dipped the quill in the inkwell, and signed her loan agreement.

"And I hear that damned gypsy tinker has been seen in town again," Martin told Mr. Howard. "I thought the marshal ran his ass out of Ellsworth two years ago.

"His prices on hard goods are quite a bit better than those at the mercantile," Callie said with a sly smile. "And he can get just about anything. I just ordered one of Mr. Singer's new-fangled machines from him at a very reasonable price and several of the girls at The Ellsworth have ordered new furniture for their rooms."

Martin's face turned a peculiar shade of purple. "What do you think of that bullshit, Ted? This bitch and her whores think they are going to put me out of business. What do you think about that?" Martin bellowed and pounded his fist on the banker's desk.

"I think the bank shouldn't plan on adding a six-hundred-forty-acre farm to its holdings," the banker mumbled as he grinned at Callie and winked.

CHAPTER 23

WHAT DO YOU THINK OF THAT?

Clayton squinted in the bright March sunshine as he plowed the garden area with his newly purchased push-plow. An old man in a tinker's wagon had stopped by and sold Clayton the plow along with some bags of seed for his spring planting.

After some hounding from Hawk, Clayton had also purchased a few pieces of iron cookware, a new broom, some laundry soap, and a washboard. The old man had taken his house chores seriously, scrubbing floors, washing windows, and dumping the chamber pots on a regular basis.

"You take them muddy boots off before you come trackin' up my clean floors, boy," Hawk yelled as he walked past from the barn where he had been tending a clutch of chicks he'd gotten from a nearby farmer's wife.

It's worse than having a damned wife.

"Yes, dear," Clayton called back.

"When ya get done turnin' up that earth, do ya think ya could tend ta tightenin' that clothesline I asked after last week? Hawk asked with his hands on his hips. "The last time I hanged sheets on it they dragged the ground."

Clayton rolled his eyes, stopped, and wiped his brow with his sleeve. "I'll get right on that, dear."

"Thank ya, boy. I wanna wash them sheets again this week," he said before disappearing into the house.

Clayton smiled to himself. Having the old man around all winter had been a delight and he'd miss him when he decided to take up his wandering again. Hawk hadn't said anything, but with the weather warming, he expected to see the old man's pack and rifle by the door any day.

Since Christmas, he and Callie had exchanged a number of letters. He enjoyed reading about her classes with the young women at The Ellsworth and the progress being made on the construction of her shop. She talked a lot about women's fashions, which he couldn't fathom, but sometimes she added a sketch to help him understand a sleeve design or a fancy apron.

It tickled Clayton that she had such grand plans for her shop. She had ordered a large piece of glass for a display window and hoped to coax some of the local women with the clothes she would display there. Clayton was skeptical, but he didn't want to dash Callie's dreams.

He'd gotten a chuckle when Callie had written that she might make a display of corsets and frillies in the window to get everyone's attention. Clayton was certain it would, but he'd warned her to go slow. This was still Kansas and the moralistic Progressives still held sway in the state.

While not coming out and saying it, Clayton had written to Callie about his deep feelings for her and hoped she might have the same for him. He awaited her reply to that letter and hoped to find one in his box when he rode into town.

As the morning wore on, Clayton finished his plowing and tightened up the clothesline.

"'Bout time ya got ta that," Hawk said when he came out to get wash water from the pump. "I've been after ya 'bout it for weeks," he grumbled.

Clayton smiled. "Oh, hush, old man. Saddle that old mule and let's ride into town."

"Town?" Hawk snapped. "I've got a bird on the stove boilin' for dumplin's. I can't go runnin' off ta town for no good reason."

"Take the bird off the stove, old man," Clayton chided, "and I'll saddle the animals. Ride into town with me and have a beer."

A smile lit up Hawk's grizzled face. "Now you're talkin' my language, boy. I ain't had me a beer in months." He carried the pail of water up the stairs. "I'll set the bird on the counter and finish boilin' it up tonight. We can have dumplin's tomorrow evenin'."

"Good idea," Clayton said with a smile. "I'll get Bessie and Dolly saddled and meet ya out front."

❧

THE RIDE into Ellsworth proved pleasant. Green buds were erupting from the tips of branches and fresh grass sprouted along the road. Birds flitted through the hedgerows, chirping with excitement as they foraged for nesting materials.

"The springtime always smells so good," Hawk said from astride his mule. "So full of fresh new promise for the year to come."

Clayton smiled as he watched a bright red cardinal rest on a branch.

I guess he picked up that philosophical streak in that Jesuit school.

"I never thought on it that way," Clayton said, "but I can see your point. When I plant those seeds in the garden, they'll sprout, bloom, and eventually give us a passel of vegetables. Them blackberry briars in that hedge, there, will bloom and make berries you can make into fat pies for me to eat. I think that's promising."

"We can make 'em up into jam to spread on biscuits too," Hawk said with a wink.

It doesn't sound like he's thinkin' on wanderin' off any time soon.

At the Post Office, Clayton found a letter waiting in his box. He carried it outside and opened it. Hawk had gone on up to The Curly Buffalo with two bits Clayton had given him for beers. He'd join the old man after he read his letter.

My Dear Clayton,

It warms my heart to receive your letters. I'm glad to know you have fond feelings for me. I do for you, as well. I think back on our kisses often. They are the best kisses I've ever had.

I've never been one to commit my feelings to paper like the women in the romances I sometimes read, but I will try. The last man I had strong feelings for hurt me very badly. I loved him, gave him my body, gave him a child, and gave him my heart. He betrayed me, cast me aside, and humiliated me in more ways than you can know. Needless to say, I am afraid to give that much again.

If I am honest with myself and with you, I think I could love you, Clayton Swift. It will take some time,

*however. I am older now and have a business to con-
sider. I've made commitments. I have a mortgage. I
cannot be the woman I was to Evan and I cannot
have a child. I know these are important things to
a man.*

*If you think you can deal with those things, then I
would love to hear it from you. If you cannot, then I
will be satisfied with being your friend.*

*Fondly,
Callie*

CLAYTON STARED at the words on the page. She said
she *could* love him. She hadn't said she *did* love him.
That was fair. He hadn't said he loved her, either.

*This whole romance thing is unfathomable. She likes me. I
like her. The kisses were great and the afternoon in bed was
fantastic. What more is there? So what if she can't have babies
anymore. We're both too old to deal with babies. Damn.*

Clayton's first inclination was to march down to
The Ellsworth House and pay her a call, but Hawk
was waiting for him in the saloon. Maybe he'd go
next door after a beer. He could certainly use one to
calm his mind.

Hawk stood at the bar, nursing a mug of beer.
"Get ya a letter today, boy?" he asked with a grin.
"Give the boy a beer," Hawk told the barman.

Clayton put a nickel on the bar and nodded at
the barman.

"So, what 'bout that letter? Did she write ya?"
Hawk emptied his mug and motioned across the bar
for another.

"Yes, she wrote me," Clayton said and took a
long swallow of the cool beer.

"An' were it all flowery and mushy with professions of her love for ya?" Hawk asked, batting his eyes in an exaggerated manner.

"Cut it out, old man or I'm gonna tell the barman here to cut you off."

Hawk frowned, then patted Clayton on the shoulder playfully. "I'm just funnin' with ya, boy." The barman set a beer in front of Hawk and the old man grabbed it and took a long swallow. "Were it a nice letter or did she tell ya to drop dead because you're a horse's ass?"

Clayton grinned. "It was a nice letter," he sighed and took another swallow.

"Does she wanna see your sorry ass again?" Hawk asked and rolled his rheumy eyes.

Clayton shrugged his broad shoulders and frowned. "I don't know, but I want to see her."

"Then go see her, boy." Hawk swallowed more beer. "Are ya scar't ta go an' see her? Women can turn on ya quick, that's for certain. One minute they're all over ya with sweet kisses an' then just like that," Hawk said and swung his hand across his throat, "you're in the outhouse with a chamber pot cracked over your noggin." He shook his gray head. "There's no rhyme nor reason ta 'em sometimes, but it's hard ta live without 'em for very long."

Clayton emptied his mug in one long swallow. "I'm gonna go see her," he said. "Can you and Bessie get home without me?"

"No worries there," Hawk told him with a too broad grin. "Go see your girl."

"That's it for him," Clayton told the barman who smiled and nodded in understanding.

"Well, what do ya think 'bout that?" Clayton heard Hawk say as he left the saloon.

Clayton was about to walk up to The Ellsworth House when he heard hammering coming from the structure next door. He stepped off the porch and crossed an empty lot to stand in front of a narrow shotgun structure with a second floor. A man with a paintbrush in his hand was stenciling something in gold on a broad pane of glass. Callie's Lady's Emporium

Through the window, Clayton could see people moving around.

"The owner in there?" Clayton asked the painter.

"Yah," he said without looking away from his work, "her and Mr. Toliver are in there arguin' about tables and counters and the like. You can go on in."

"Thanks," Clayton said and pushed open the newly painted six-panel door.

Callie stood inside with her hair tied in the back with a ribbon. Her feet were spread in a defiant stance and her hands rested on her hips. "I want the cutting table all the way in the back, two display tables near the front door, and the counter here in the middle of the wall between the side windows."

The man, presumably her building contractor, Mr. Toliver, rolled his eyes. "I'd put the counter to the front and the tables to the middle of the room. It makes more sense."

"I don't want the counter to block the display window," Callie explained, "and if the counter is in the middle here, I can watch the whole store, front, and back."

Toliver threw up his hands in resignation. "You're the boss," he huffed and walked away from Callie.

"I wish you'd remember that," Callie mumbled as she turned to see Clayton grinning down at her.

"Labor troubles?" he asked.

Callie rolled her eyes and rubbed her hands on her paint-stained apron. "I'm sure I'll come in tomorrow or the next day and the counter will be right up there." She pointed toward the big window.

"This is a great space," Clayton said, glancing around the store that smelled of freshly milled lumber and paint.

Callie's face brightened with the compliment and she took his hand. "Let me show you around," she said, tugging him toward the back of the store. "You've already seen the display window, of course, and I gather you heard where I want my counter." She pointed to a curtained closet-like structure. "That is the dressing room and those shelves in the corner will have hat stands on them for the latest bonnets of the season."

"What do whores need with bonnets?" he asked with a nervous grin. "They don't wear them in bed."

Callie slapped his arm. "They have to go out sometime."

"I suppose you're right," he said. "What's back there?" he asked, pointing to the back of the building.

"That will be my work area and storage space for my rolls of fabric."

Clayton walked back to inspect the area. A flight of stairs led up. "Where does this go?"

"That," Callie said, taking Clayton's hand, "is the very best part." She led him up the stairs and through a door into an open space with windows at both ends.

"What's so great about an attic?" he asked, ducking his head because of the slope of the roofline.

"This," she said, sweeping her arm around the space, "will be my new living quarters. I'm putting a cookstove, some cupboards, and a dry sink on this end for a kitchen area and a bed, vanity, and wardrobe on the other end for my bedroom. I'll have a big comfortable chair and table for doing work in the evenings." Callie grinned up at Clayton. "Well, won't this be better than me living next door?"

Clayton stared around in dismay. She'd thought of everything. With a set-up like this, Callie had everything she needed; her business, her home, and her independence.

"Yah," he sighed, "this is real nice."

Callie put a hand on Clayton's. "What's wrong? I thought you wanted me out of The Ellsworth."

"I did ... I do," he stammered. "I just didn't think it would be like this."

"What do you mean?" she asked uneasily. "Like what?"

"All alone here," he said, staring around the empty space. "Do you think that's safe for a woman?"

"The doors will be locked when the store isn't open," Callie said confidently and shrugged her shoulders. "Lots of women live alone."

Clayton pulled her into his arms. "But none of them is my woman," he said and kissed her.

"Your woman?" Callie whispered and peered up into his eyes.

"If you want to be, that is," Clayton said uneasily as he ran his strong hand up and down her back.

"You read my letter?"

"I did."

"And what do you think?" Callie asked and rested her head on his chest.

"I think you're a strong-willed woman," he said. "You made all of this happen." He swept his hand around the room. "Not many could have." He kissed her again before taking a deep breath and continuing. "I know you have obligations now and I respect that. I have obligations too. I have fences to string for cattle and I'm thinkin' on sowing more rye for hay in one-quarter of the property." He pulled her close and held her tight. "We're both gonna be busy people, but I think I'm willing to give it a go if you are."

Callie stared up into his eyes and smiled. "So am I," she sighed and took a step back. "It's not going to bother you that I'll be doing business with the disreputable women of Ellsworth?"

Clayton chuckled. "At least you won't be living with them anymore." His eyes drifted to the far end of the empty space where Callie said her bedroom would be. "When's that furniture supposed to be getting' here?"

CHAPTER 24
FRESH PROMISE

Callie was giddy with excitement. The wagon with her bolts of cloth had finally arrived and it was being unloaded. She had ordered four ten-yard bolts of silk for camisoles and bloomers, five bolts of plain white cotton for the same, as well as for petticoats, nightdresses, and dressing gowns.

Callie watched as the young man lined the back wall with colorful spring shades of brushed cotton for day dresses and Sunday frocks. Richer hues of summer-weight wool would become suits and Callie pictured elegant parlor dresses made from the jewel-tone satins.

I'm so excited. I can't wait to get started and fill my shop with beautiful things.

Wire dress forms stood in the back waiting to be draped in finery and boxes of laces and ribbons were stacked in the back ready to adorn that finery.

"What's going on in here?" Lil asked when she came through the door, her cane tapping the wood floor as she walked.

"I got my first fabric order," Callie gushed. "Isn't it just beautiful?"

Lil walked over and fingered some sapphire-blue

satin. "I may have to put dibs on some of this," she said with a raised silver brow. "Do you have plans for all of this already?"

"Every bit of it," Callie sighed. "I want to have stock in the shop before the girls show back up in town for cattle season."

"You're gonna be working 'round the clock, girl. It's a good thing you have a bed upstairs," Lil said with a grin, pointing up to Callie's newly furnished living quarters.

"I finally figured out how to thread the Singer," Callie sighed, "and I think I have the pedal figured out. If it's all they make it out to be in the periodicals, I should be able to seam up a dress in a day."

Lil rolled her eyes skeptically. "I'll believe that when I see it and hope the damned seams hold. I can't say as I trust a machine to do stitch work." She ran her hand over the seam on her tight bodice. "I need a good sturdy seam to keep all this in place."

Callie smiled as she went to the machine and picked up some squares of fabric. She handed it to Lil. "I've been doing some test runs. The seams appear to be plenty strong. This bobbin thing is like running a double stitched seam."

Lil took the fabric, studied it carefully, and tugged at the seam. "Looks like it might work," she said, but Callie saw doubt in the old woman's eyes.

Someone knocked on the door. Callie opened it and found Carl Martin, Ted Howard from the bank, and Judge Sterling standing outside.

"What can I do for you gentlemen today?" Callie asked cordially.

"Are you open for business yet, Mrs. Jamison?" the white-headed Judge asked.

Callie studied the group and saw the banker give her a slight shake of his balding head.

"Not quite yet," Callie said. "I have the building, but I still have to make my stock."

"We're here on behalf of the Ellsworth City Council," the beak-nosed Martin announced, "to see your business license."

"Business license?" Callie inquired. "What's that?"

"Ignorant woman doesn't even know what she needs in order to conduct business in Ellsworth," he sneered.

Judge Sterling glared at Martin. "I have the forms here for you to fill out, Mrs. Jamison." He reached into his leather satchel and pulled out several sheets of paper. "Fill them out and return them to me at the courthouse with the fee and we'll issue you your license to conduct business in Ellsworth."

Callie saw Martin's mouth fall open and he glared at the Judge.

I wonder what that's all about?

"What kind of fee?" Lil chimed in.

"It's twenty-dollars," smirked Martin. "And it's due and payable every year if you plan to sell your wares here in our fair city."

"More political thievery," Lil snorted.

"We really don't need any comments from the likes of you, madam," Martin scolded.

"Oh, really?" Lil said and took a step toward the surly man.

Callie touched Lil's arm. "It's all right, Lil. I can handle this."

Martin craned his neck to peer into Callie's back room where the young man had just finished stacking the final bolts of fabric. "I suppose you have the twenty dollars needed after all your extravagant expenditures," he snorted as he ran a hand over one of the finely sanded and varnished display tables."

The banker stepped forward and handed Callie a blank bank draft. "You can fill this out for the twenty-dollars, Mrs. Jamison. You have ample funds left in your account to cover the license fee."

Martin's eyes went wide. "What are you two idiots doing?" he hissed. "I'm trying to keep this bitch from opening her doors and you seem to be bending over backward to help her do just that." Martin scowled at the two men. "Has she been bending over for the two of you?" Martin hissed. "Has she been spreading her legs for you to gain your favor?"

Lil shook loose of Callie's hand. "I've had about enough of this foul-mouthed little bastard," she hissed as she stepped forward and took hold of Martin's ear.

Martin squealed as Lil twisted hard and pulled Martin toward the door. "Get your filthy hand off me, you, fat old tart."

"Fat old tart, huh?" Lil hissed as she pulled Martin to the door. "Get out of here you skinny, rude, little weasel." She used her hip to open the door and shoved Martin out so hard he stumbled and landed on his behind in the mud of Front Street. "And don't come back. You're not welcome here."

Lil walked back, dusting her hands off as though she'd just thrown out some rubbish. "I assume you gentlemen are not of the same mind as the little weasel?" she asked, cocking her head toward the door.

"No, ma'am," Judge Sterling replied with a charming smile. He turned to Callie. "If you can fill out the form now and sign it, we'll be on our way and let the Council know you're in perfect compliance with all the city ordinances."

"I will," she said and took the papers to the counter where she had an ink well and pen. "This will just take a minute," she said and began answering the required questions.

"If you'll hand me that draft," Howard told her, "I'll fill it out and you can sign it."

Callie smiled and handed the banker the slip of paper. "I appreciate all your help, gentlemen," Callie said with tears of appreciation in her eyes.

Howard patted Callie's arm. "I'm just looking out for the Stockholders' interests. If you can't open, you can't sell your goods. If you can't sell your goods, you can't pay your mortgage."

"I certainly appreciate it," Callie said again. "I've got lots of work to do before I open my doors for business."

Callie finished the paperwork, signed the draft, and handed it all to Judge Sterling. "When are you planning your Grand Opening?" he asked.

"I'm hoping for the first of June," Callie sighed, "but I have a lot of sewing and staging to do before then."

"Don't worry, sugar," Lil said and patted Callie's shoulder. "Me and the girls will help with everything. Your shop will be ready to go when the seasonal girls hit the town."

CHAPTER 25

THE OPENING IS GRAND

The first Saturday in June dawned bright and warm. Clayton woke beside Callie in her bedroom above the store.

"Did you get any sleep at all?" Clayton asked and rolled over to kiss her cheek.

"Not much," she said as she stretched and yawned. "Maybe a couple of hours. I was just too nervous, going over and over details in my mind."

"I'll put on some coffee," he said and kissed her again.

"Could we go to The Flat Iron for breakfast? I could eat your horse."

"Dolly wouldn't like that at all," Clayton said with a grin as he pulled up his trousers. "The Flat Iron it is."

Callie dressed for her day in a lavender cotton day dress trimmed with white crocheted lace, pearl buttons, and ribbons a shade darker than the fabric. She brushed her hair up and tied it with a piece of the ribbon, slipped into her white boots and gloves.

"You look beautiful, Callie," Clayton said, staring at her.

"Will you help me with the apron?" Callie asked

and wrapped the gathered apron around her slim waist. "Tie it with a big bow so that the ruffled lace bunches up on my behind."

Clayton screwed his face up in confusion. "I'll never understand why a woman would want to make her ass look bigger than it is."

Callie grinned and shrugged her narrow shoulders. "I can't explain the whys of current fashions," she sighed, "I just choose the prettiest fabric and sew them together."

"You did a fine job with this one," Clayton complemented and kissed her again. "It's beautiful."

"Thank you," Callie said and kissed Clayton on the cheek in return. "Come see what we did with the shop," she said excitedly and tugged him down the stairs. "We worked on it all night. I think I'm going to take the curtain down off the window before we leave for breakfast, so people can get a look at it before we open."

It astonished Clayton to see what Callie had accomplished in just a few months. Tables were piled with folded lady's undergarments in a variety of colors and fabrics. Dress forms stood around the room displaying frilly dressing gowns, day dresses, suits, and fancy parlor gowns. One form displayed a lace-trimmed corset cinched up over a silk camisole and bloomers. Bonnets trimmed with silk flowers and feathers sat atop wire hat stands.

Two dress forms stood behind the draped window. One wore a ruby-red satin gown with a matching bonnet the other wore an emerald-green dressing gown trimmed in thick rows of black lace around the collar and at the cuffs.

Callie was happy to see a group of women waiting for the unveiling of the window. Eyes grew wide and hands flew to mouths at the sight of the luxurious garments presented.

"Let's get some food," Callie said with a beaming smile. "I think it's going to be a busy day."

Two women rushed to the door when Callie opened it. "How much is the green dressing gown?" one woman asked. "Can we come in now?" asked another as she reached for the door.

"We'll be open at nine," Callie said with a broad smile. "I need some coffee and breakfast first."

Clayton took her hand as they walked toward The Flat Iron. "I think Callie's Lady's Emporium is going to be a grand success, my love."

"I hope so," Callie sighed. "I have a mortgage."

"I don't think the bank has anything to worry about," he said with a smile.

And neither do I. I'm sure my ranch is perfectly safe.

Inside The Flat Iron, tables were full. Mr. Jenkins greeted them warmly, but Callie saw sneers on the faces of people sitting in a large group. The Martins were amongst the group.

Callie's mouth watered with the aromas of coffee and frying bacon. Mr. Jenkins brought them cups and a pot of coffee.

"I just got in a bucket of fresh maple syrup," Mr. Jenkins said with a broad grin, "so the missus is making her delicious buttermilk pancakes today."

"That sounds good," Clayton said. "I'll have a plate with bacon and a couple of eggs."

"Me too," added Callie.

Mr. Jenkins's eyes darted to the table where the Martins sat. "I know this has been a bone of contention down at the church," he whispered, "but Mrs. Jenkins would like to come visit your store today."

Callie grinned. "She's more than welcome. If it

would make her feel more comfortable, have her come up the alley and through the back door." Callie winked. "I'll leave it unlocked."

"I'll let her know," he said with a grin. He patted Callie's shoulder appreciatively. "Thank you, Miss Callie. She's been fretting over it some, but really wants to see your wares." Mr. Jenkins turned and walked briskly to the kitchen.

"That back door just might be your private entrance for the curious town ladies you hope to attract," Clayton said with a raised brow and an impish grin.

Callie rolled her eyes. "I was just thinking the same thing."

"I'll clear a nice path for you from the back door to the alley when we get back," Clayton said.

"Thank you," she said with a giggle. "It will be interesting to see which door gets more foot traffic."

"I suppose I'll have to install one of them little bells on the back door too," he said and chuckled and sipped his coffee.

"Mornin', sugar," Lil said from the aisle. "Mind if we join you?"

"Not at all," Callie said and moved around to the chair closer to Clayton. Lil and Mae took the other two.

"You get any sleep last night?" Lil asked as she spread a linen napkin over the skirt of her new blue cotton suit.

Mae wore a frilly green frock trimmed in white lace and pearl buttons.

"You ladies look lovely today," Clayton said as he studied Lil over his coffee cup.

Could this really be the famous Lil Hawk told me about? The woman who sacrificed her virtue to save her family and her town?

"Why thank you, sugar," Lil said with a smile on her rouged lips. "I don't know as this old body is one to show off Callie's talents, but I'm not one to turn down a new dress when one is offered."

"Me neither," Mae added, running a petite hand down the cotton sleeve of her dress. "This is the prettiest dress I've owned since my ma passed. She always made us a new dress for Christmas and one at Easter time." The young woman brushed a tear from her freckled cheek.

Mr. Jenkins took note of the new customers at Callie's table and brought more cups and coffee. The women ordered pancakes as well. He brought out their plates together and everyone enjoyed the hot buttery pancakes drowned in warm maple syrup.

"I'm so glad Isaac the Tinker has Ellsworth on his route again," Mr. Jenkins said with a sideways glance at the Martins. "He's the only one who can or will get this quality syrup."

"He was out by my place and sold me a new push plow and some other goods," Clayton said. "His prices are very reasonable."

Lil raised a brow. "I never knew Isaac came to Ellsworth before," she said. "I knew him from Abilene and asked him to come when somebody," she jerked her head toward the Martins' table, "decided he didn't want to do business with the likes of us living at The Ellsworth."

Jenkins' eyes went wide, and he grinned. "So, you're the one I have to thank for this? Your breakfast is on the house." He put a hand on Lil's shoulder. "My wife is thrilled to have someone to mend her pots again," his eyes darted back to the other table, "even if I have to take them to the town limits."

"The town limits?" Clayton said as he popped a bite into his mouth.

"Some people in town made it impossible for Isaac to do business inside the town limits—licenses and fees," he said in an exasperated tone, "So, Isaac can only conduct business out there past the town limit sign."

Lil grinned and winked at Callie. "Maybe he should build a store."

Clayton smiled along with the old woman. He'd heard from Callie how Lil had handled Martin.

A little competition would really frost the bastard's cake and I'd be more than happy to help the tinker build the place.

"It would be a boon to this town if he could," Mr. Jenkins sighed, "a real boon."

"Isaac and his wife are getting too old to be traveling about in that old wagon," Lil said. "I'll talk to them about putting up a storefront out there."

"I know plenty of folks in this town—me included-- who'd welcome another mercantile."

Behind them, chairs scooted and were knocked across the wood floor and they heard feet stomping toward the door. Their heads turned to see the Martins storming out of the building.

"Didn't even pay for their damned meal," Mr. Jenkins hissed and turned to begin picking up chairs.

⚜

"CAN YOU BELIEVE THIS?" Callie gasped after she, Clayton, and Lil had counted the coin in the cash box a third time.

"I knew you were gonna be a hit with the seasonal women," Lil said with a broad smile on her tired face.

They'd opened the store to a clamoring crowd at nine that morning and hadn't shut and locked the doors until after seven that evening, and they'd had to shoo women out in order to do it.

After Mrs. Jenkins's visit through the rear door, several other local ladies had used the same entrance to take a peek into Callie's Lady's Emporium.

It had been a long day and Lil had been a huge help, sitting at the counter, taking orders, and collecting money.

Callie gazed around the room at the empty dress forms and tables devoid of the garments folded upon them that morning.

"It's gonna take me another three months to restock all of this," she said with a happy sigh.

"But you made more than enough today to pay off your mortgage," Clayton said enthusiastically.

Callie grinned. "Not after I take out the cost of materials to resupply all of this," she said, sweeping her hand around the room with its empty tables and denuded dress forms.

"Oh," he said, staring around the room, "I guess you're right."

This place looks like a herd of cattle ran through it on their way to water after a long dry spell. I don't know how she's gonna do it.

NOBODY IS PERFECTLY SAFE

Three men bellied up to the bar in The Curly Buffalo Saloon. They all ordered a whiskey. Their fine clothes didn't reflect their rough countenances.

"We have to do something about that rabid bitch of yours, Jamison." The thinnest of them growled. "She and her gaggle of sluts are bound and determined to put me out of business."

"Humph," the man in a tailored brown suede jacket and cowboy's hat groaned. "I just got served a notice yesterday from Judge Sterling, ordering me to pay half the cunny's mortgage on her damned store."

He tipped up the shot glass and emptied it in one swallow. "It was bad enough that I had to pay Caine here five dollars a month to keep her housed in his whorehouse. Now I have to pay four-fifty because she's livin' above her damned store." The rancher swallowed a second whiskey. "I didn't mind paying Caine, but it frosts my bollocks to give my money to that damned banker."

The tallest man with a scarred face frowned and

added, "She taught the gaggle of sluts how to read and do ciphers. Now they are demanding *full accountings of all transactions in writing.*" He shook his head as he pushed his glass toward the barman for a refill. "She's been nothing but trouble since day one," he snarled and rubbed a finger over a healing cut on his left cheek.

"Well, what are we gonna do about her?" the skinny man snapped.

"If she didn't have that damned store," the rancher snarled, "We'd both be the better for it, Martin."

"I'm not sure I want her back in The Ellsworth," the tall man hissed, but I'd surely like to use my belt tickle her pretty white hide again." He lowered his hand to his crotch and gave it a squeeze. "That ass ain't virgin no more, Evan," he told the rancher with a chuckle. "It was nice 'n tight."

"Did she squeal?" the rancher asked with a grin.

"Like a poked sow," Caine said with a chuckle.

"Am I the only one here that hasn't poked the bitch?" the skinny man asked and shook his head.

"We should all three go over there some night, give her a poke she'll never forget, and then burn the place down with her in it," the rancher said with an evil grin.

"Now there's an idea I could get behind," the skinny man said and hunched his crotch into the bar. "My wife only wants to do it one way—on her back, fast asleep."

"Callie always had some sweet cunny," the rancher sighed and swallowed another glass of whiskey, "but the things she could do with her mouth," he grinned, closed his eyes, and made as if to shiver.

"Her cunny was dry, and her mouth wasn't anything special," the tall man said, "but that virgin asshole—hmm," he shivered too. "I could surely go for that again."

"Well," the skinny man said, "let's make a plan. You've got my cock hard thinking about hearing the bitch scream while that damned store burns down around her."

"What about that big cowboy who's always by her side now?" the rancher asked. "I hear tell he's sharin' her bed up there in that store. I wonder if Sterling knows about that. Maybe he'd resend that order and make the cowboy pokin' her pay the four-fifty."

"We can deal with a stupid cowboy," the tall, scarred man said. "Nobody's gonna say anything about two burned up bodies in a whore's clothing store."

"Come on," the skinny man said and slapped the others on the back, "let's walk down to Callie's Lady's Emporium and make a plan."

The three men walked out of The Curly Buffalo Saloon chuckling together. They paid no mind to the shabby little gray-headed man at the end of the bar who'd been listening to every word.

❧

CALLIE STOOD in front of the teller's window with a concerned furrow on her brow. "I don't understand, Mr. Rykard," she said, staring down at her unfolded contract, "Mr. Howard told me I could pay this off at any time without having to pay all this interest."

The thin, redheaded teller smiled down at Callie. "You must have misunderstood, Mrs. Jamison," he said in a condescending tone. "The bank makes its money by charging interest on loans. Your payoff is one-thousand-eighty dollars," he said, pointing to the underlined amount on her contract.

"May I help you, Mrs. Jamison?" Mr. Howard asked, stepping out of his office.

"I … I think we have this settled, Mr. Howard, sir," the teller mumbled as he hurriedly folded Callie's contract and slid it out of the way.

"Mrs. Jamison?" Howard persisted.

"I wanted to pay off my loan," Callie said, "but this young man says I owe more than I thought."

"Is that so?" Howard said and reached across the teller to retrieve the folded contract. He unfolded it. "Your pay off amount is right here," he said pointing to a number on her amortization schedule that read: Five-hundred-four dollars and twenty cents. Howard turned to the teller.

"Is this the amount you quoted the lady?"

"I … eh … well … eh," Rykard stammered.

"He told me I owed the *total* amount of the loan with all the interest a thousand and eighty dollars," Callie said with her eyes darting between Howard and the nervous teller.

Callie watched the banker's face turn red. "I'll finish this, Mr. Rykard," Howard said, pushing the man aside. "Go wait for me in my office."

"Penny," the banker called to his receptionist, "pull the files on all the loans Mr. Rykard has taken payoffs on in the past year."

"Yes, sir," the young woman replied with a grin tugging at the corners of her mouth as she watched Rykard walk, slump-shouldered into Howard's office and close the door.

"Well, Mrs. Jamison," Howard said, clearing his

throat nervously, "I guess your grand opening went well if you are ready to pay off your loan already."

"Yes, sir," Callie said with a smile, "it certainly did."

"Are you certain you want to pay it off completely?" Howard asked. "You could pay it down some, and we could keep a line of credit open for you."

Callie's eyes darted to the office where Rykard waited for his boss.

That man was trying to steal from me. I'm sure of it.

"I think I'd be more comfortable paying off the loan, Mr. Howard and opening an account I can draw from to pay for my orders."

"Absolutely," the banker said with a smile.

Callie counted out the funds, slid them across the marble counter, and waited for Mr. Howard to stamp her contract paid in full. "And should I need another loan?"

"Your credit is good here, madam. You've more than proven your business is a viable one."

"Thank you, Mr. Howard," Callie said, tucked the contract into her bag, and shook the banker's sweaty hand.

As she opened the door to leave the bank, Callie heard the door to Howard's office slam behind her.

"AND JUST WHAT the hell were you about out there with Mrs. Jamison, Rykard?" Howard stormed as he dropped into his chair.

"I don't know what you're talking about, sir," the skinny teller said indignantly.

"You were trying to cheat that woman out of better than five hundred dollars," Howard accused.

"Come now, sir," Rykard said with a sly grin,

"everybody knows she's no better than a filthy whore and a foolish woman. There's no harm in cheating a whore out of her ill-gained goods and a woman has no place in the business world."

Howard sat, staring open-mouthed at his son-in-law. He tapped a finger on the pile of files Penny, one of his daughters, had gathered for him. "And when I go visit all of these customers, how many of them am I going to find have overpaid on their loans, Brian?"

"None of them," the man replied, staring at the stack of files. "Well, maybe one or two, but they were too stupid to know the difference and deserved it," the teller said.

"Oh, my god," the banker breathed with his hand going to his mouth. "Get out of my bank," Howard yelled as he jumped to his feet and pointed to the door.

"But … but how am I going to support Deborah and the children?" Rykard gasped.

"You should have thought about that before you started stealing from my customers," Howard seethed and opened the door. "Now get the hell out and when I find out who you've bilked out of their hard-earned money, I'll be turning it all over to the marshal for prosecution."

Howard walked the trembling man through the empty lobby and to the door. "Thank you, Penny, for bringing the situation with him and Mrs. Jamison to my attention."

The young woman nodded her head and turned to go back to her desk. "Mind things while I'm out, dear," he said and went into his office for the pile of loan files.

"You want me to run the bank, Father?" Penny asked wide-eyed.

"I have every confidence in you, girl," he said with a nervous grin. "I've recently acquired a new appreciation of the capabilities of women in business." He settled his hat upon his head and left the bank with the stack of files in his arms.

CHAPTER 27

NOW IT'S TIME TO PAY

Clayton and Callie sat in The Flat Iron, enjoying plates of Mrs. Jenkins' fried chicken with mashed potatoes, cream gravy, and biscuits.

"I should really get back to the shop," Callie sighed. "I finally got part of that second shipment of fabric in and I should be cutting." She emptied her coffee cup. "I have women waiting for orders they placed, and I need to refill my tables."

"You and Lil have been doing a fine job," Clayton said. "The place looks almost as nice as it did the day you opened."

Callie rolled her eyes. "Not even close."

Lil had been helping Callie to use up the fabric from her first order and the tables now had a variety of items stacked on them and the dress forms had been redressed.

When Callie discovered Lil's fine embroidery hand, she hired the woman to add enhancements to many of her garments. Simple white cotton camisoles now had pretty, embroidered scrollwork around the necklines, sleeves, and hems. A bit of pretty embroidery added elegance and Callie wanted her shop to become known for quality and elegance at a reasonable price.

"You're practically selling things as fast as you put them out on display," he said, taking her hand.

"We must find a better eating establishment, my dear," Clayton heard someone say as they passed, "they don't seem to care what sort of trash they let in here."

He saw Callie scowling after the man. The well-dressed stocky, older man looked familiar, but Clayton couldn't place the man.

"Who is that?" he asked.

"That's Evan Jamison," Callie sighed, "my former husband."

Clayton gave the man a closer look.

Where do I know him from? He looks so familiar.

When the man picked up a glass of water and put it to his lips, it dawned on Clayton where he'd seen the man.

That's the ass who was talking about Callie in the saloon. Of course, he knew what Callie liked in bed—she was married to him for ten years. What a fool I am.

"What is it?" Callie asked when she felt Clayton tightening his grip painfully around her hand.

"Oh," he said and released his grip. "I'm so sorry. Did I hurt you?"

Callie rubbed her hand, "No, I'm fine. What got you so riled all of a sudden?"

"I owe you such an apology, Callie," he said, glaring across the room at Evan Jamison.

"I told you it's fine," she said and forked up the last of her potatoes.

"Not about that," Clayton said with a frown and went on to explain about the night in the Curly Buf-falo after their first kiss. "I feel like such an ass now."

"You're not the ass, Clayton," she said, scowling at her former husband. "Evidently he's been saying things like that about me all over Ellsworth since our divorce."

"You don't say?" Clayton hissed. "I should go over there and beat his damned face in."

Callie grabbed Clayton's hand. "Don't. It's not worth it." Callie took a deep breath. "I don't know when, but Evan Jamison will get what's coming to him."

A breeze caused by the door opening and closing ruffled Callie's skirts.

"I should really be getting back to the shop," Callie sighed. "I have so much work to do."

The fussing of an infant drew her attention and Callie turned her head to see Polly Hardin marching determinedly between tables with a squirming bundle in her arms.

"Maybe that day is here," Callie whispered to Clayton as she stepped out of Polly's way.

Callie watched the girl, who'd filled out some from her pregnancy, march up to Evan and shove the mound of blankets into his arms. "Here you go, Evan," Polly shouted for everyone in the busy café to hear. "Here's the son you wanted so badly." She turned to leave, but when she saw Callie, she turned back to the wide-eyed man and said, "I named him Cal, by the way." She winked at Callie as she stormed back toward the door.

"What do you expect me to do?" he called after the girl, "I don't want this little bastard."

Men and women alike glared at Evan as he rushed after the departing girl with the infant squalling in his arms.

"Oh, my," Clayton said with a giggle.

"Oh, my, indeed," Callie said as she took Clayton's arm.

"This is not amusing," the woman who'd come in with Evan hissed at Callie.

Callie recognized her as the new schoolteacher Evan had been with in Martins. "No, it isn't," Callie replied. "Evan is responsible for the futures of both those children," she said, referring to both Polly and her baby.

"Evan swears he never coupled with that girl," the woman said defiantly.

"Evan is a liar," Callie called back to her, "I caught them rutting in the bushes, myself. Ask him about the day I went berry picking last summer." Callie grinned at the red-faced woman. "You should really reread that morality clause in your employment contract, dear. It says something in there about being seen out in public with disreputable types. Evan Jamison is about as disreputable as they come here in Ellsworth, in my way of thinking." Callie turned back and took Clayton's arm.

"That was harsh," Clayton whispered into Callie's hair.

Evan walked back through the door with the infant screaming in his arms. Callie stopped and brushed the blankets off the child's red face.

"Take this thing, Callie," Evan said pushing the bundle toward her.

Callie stepped back. "I'm happy for you, Evan. Your son looks just like you. Nobody will deny he's yours," Callie said in a loud, clear voice. "But I think he's hungry." Callie stepped around her former husband and walked out into the warm, summer evening.

"Now," Callie said with a grin, "*that* was harsh."

Clayton chuckled. "Indeed, it was. Remind me never to fall on your bad side, Miss Callie."

Callie smiled up at him. "You really don't have to stay with me tonight," she said as they strolled together back to her building, "I'm going to be up working for hours."

A mule hee-hawed somewhere in the distance and a horse whinnied in reply. Callie peered up at the bright stars twinkling in the inky sky. "It's such a beautiful night. I'm going to open all the windows and enjoy the breeze while I work."

"I don't mind staying. I want to make sure you're safe."

Clayton had been staying with Callie since Hawk had come home with the story about the men talking in the saloon. From his descriptions of the men, he'd suspect one to be Martin from the mercantile and one to be Caine from The Ellsworth.

Could the third man be Jamison? He could be the man Hawk described. If it is, I don't think he'll be out causing trouble tonight.

"I think the third man Hawk described could be your husband, Callie. Hawk said the man was complaining about having to pay your rent. That would be him, wouldn't it?" Clayton asked.

"I seriously doubt Evan would be in on a plan to assault and kill me, Clayton."

"He had no problem assaulting your reputation in the Curly Buffalo with the place packed with men listening to his filth."

"Evan is a loudmouth," Callie sighed, "especially after he's had a few whiskeys, but he's never been violent."

They walked up to the front door and Callie unlocked it. She opened the heavy wood door and they stepped inside. The room smelled of new lumber, paint, and lamp oil. Clayton pushed the door shut and took Callie into his arms. "I think I should stay," he said, bent, and kissed her passionately.

Callie wrapped her arms around his neck and twined her fingers into his silky shoulder-length hair. She returned the kiss, but when her nipples began to throb with desire, she pushed away. "I think you should go," she said with a smile. "I have so much work to do and you and your kisses are a distraction."

Clayton smiled and took a deep breath. "Dolly's not gonna be happy about riding home in the dark."

"Tell Dolly I'm sorry, but I have so damn much work to do." Callie stepped away from Clayton, who stood frowning at her. "I've got all this new fabric and trim to sort through," she said and began walking toward the back where her cutting table stood along with bolts of cloth and several boxes.

Clayton followed and stopped when she did to boost the flame on the lamp she'd lit before leaving for supper. "Come look at all this," she said and continued to the back of the long, narrow building.

Callie lit another lamp to illuminate her workspace. "Damn," she hissed, "I thought sure I bolted this before I left." She went to the door and slid the heavy iron bolt into the frame. When she tested the knob, she smiled. "Locked up tight," she sighed. "I guess I just forgot to slide the bolt before I left."

"You need to be more vigilant," Clayton scolded.

Callie rolled her eyes and put her hands on his chest. "You need to get going, so I can get to work," Callie said and pushed him toward the front.

"Oh, all right," he said resignedly, "but I'll be back in a few days to see how you're doing."

"I'll be cutting and sewing," she said with a giggle, "that's what I'll be doing."

Clayton frowned but bent and kissed her again. "I love you, Callie," he whispered, "and I think it'd kill me to lose you."

I've never said those words to a woman in my entire life, not even to my mother.

"I love you too, Clay," Callie sighed, "and I don't say those words lightly."

CHAPTER 28
BE MORE VIGILANT

Callie strolled back into her workroom, carrying her lamp. She wore a broad smile on her face.

He said he loves me. I can't believe it. He loves me. I feel like a silly schoolgirl again.

She set the lamp on her worktable and stepped toward the waiting rolls of fabric. As Callie reached for a roll of pink silk, someone grabbed her hair from behind and yanked her off her feet.

What the hell! Not again!

"Did you really think you were gonna get away with shaming me like you did, Callie?" Caine growled, hovering over her with his hideous grinning face. "We're gonna teach you a lesson tonight that you're never gonna forget."

We? What the hell is he going on about now?

"Get her out of those ridiculous clothes, Caine, I want to see what you and Evan have been going on about all this time." Callie recognized Carl Martin's voice.

Caine leered down at her as he grabbed her dress at the neck and yanked. Buttons flew and she heard them ping against the wall and floor.

I've had about enough of this bullshit.

"Let go of me, you ugly bastard," Callie screamed and clawed.

Caine slapped her hard. Callie saw pinpoints of light before her eyes with the jarring slap.

"I see you need another lesson on who's a boss and who's not." Caine shoved Callie down onto the table. "Hold her down, Martin, while I take off my belt."

Oh, no, you don't. I've had all of this I'm going to take.

Martin grabbed for Callie as Caine stepped back, fumbling with his belt. Callie screamed as loudly as she could, then rolled away from the men across the wide table and landed on the floor.

"Damnit, Martin," Caine growled, "this was your fucking idea in the first place. Go get her."

"Let's just smash the damned lamp and burn the place," Martin grumbled. "That's all I really wanted to do."

"Yah," Caine growled, "but I want to stripe her hide again and poke her asshole."

"You're a real piece of work, Caine," Martin sneered.

"I wanna fuck her," Caine snapped, "but you wanna tie her to her bed and burn her alive. What kinda man does that make you, Martin?"

"Let's just get her and drag her ass up the stairs to her bed and get this over with," Martin barked at the big man.

As the men came around the table, Callie rolled beneath it. She watched their ankles moving and her mind raced. She needed a weapon. Where were her fabric shears? If she could get her hands on those maybe she would have a fighting chance against the bastards.

Where did I leave my damned shears? They're probably

over on the Singer or out front on the counter where Lil was working.

"Come on out and take your medicine like a good girl," Caine said and snapped his leather belt. He bent and reached for Callie beneath the table.

Callie kicked out with her booted foot and caught Caine on the temple with her heel and he jumped back. Her momentum sent her to the other side of the table where Martin waited to grab her.

"I got her," Martin called to Caine, "I got her." He took a page from Caine's book and grabbed Callie by the hair.

"Get out from under there, Callie," Martin hissed. "You've got some atoning to do for your sins against the good men of Ellsworth."

"What good men?" Callie snarled. "I've yet to meet one."

"Not even that cowboy you been spreadin' your legs for of late?" Caine sneered. "Ain't he a good man?"

"Yah, but he's not from Ellsworth."

"A matter of semantics," Martin said and pulled Callie to her feet by her hair. "You understand big words, don't you, former schoolteacher," he whispered in her ear, and then ran a hand over her bare shoulder and down over the breasts Caine had bared when he ripped open her dress.

Martin grinned up at Caine. "Maybe I will have a little taste of this before we set this place on fire."

Callie stomped on Martin's foot with all her strength. "Not if I have anything to say about it," she hissed and tried to wrench herself out of his wiry grasp.

"You, goddamned bitch," Martin roared with pain and pushed Callie away and onto the hard tabletop. He reached down, grabbed her skirt, and pulled what was left of her dress and petticoat off.

He reached down to the button on his trousers. "I'm gonna fuck your mouth, your ass, and your damned cunny, bitch before I douse your bed in lamp oil and set it on fire." He pointed a bony finger in Callie's face. "Then I'm gonna stand back and whack-off while I listen to you scream."

"You're one sick son-of-a-bitch, Martin," Caine said with a chuckle. "Let's get this bitch upstairs so we can begin the fun," he said as he brought his belt down to lash across Callie's naked belly.

Callie heard the clicking of a rifle being racked. "I think you're both assholes," someone said from the doorway, surprising both Martin and Caine.

Callie twisted her head around to see a weathered old man standing with a rifle at his shoulder. "Now let the lady up so's she kin cover 'erself proper."

"This is no concern of yours, mister," Caine said and turned to face the old man. "You should be on your way so we can finish having our fun."

"Nope," the old man said and squeezed the trigger. Callie flinched with the loud report in the confined space. The bullet pierced Caine between the eyes and blew out the back of his skull, sending blood and brain-matter splattering against the wall before Caine toppled to the floor.

I hope none of that got on my new fabric.

Callie rolled off the table and grabbed for what was left of her tattered clothes.

"You gonna be a bit more reasonable, fella?" the old man asked Martin.

The trembling mercantile owner grabbed Callie in an attempt to use her as a shield.

"Guess not," the old man said, racked the rifle again, and fired.

The bullet took the top of Martin's head off, splattering gore on the wall beside Callie's new rolls of fabric.

"Sorry 'bout the mess, missy, the old man said apologetically when he saw her staring at the red and gray goo sliding down the wall.

Callie flinched and clutched the rags that had once been her clothes to her as the front door crashed open and Clayton stormed into the room.

"What the hell's been going on here?" he stammered as he took in the scene.

"Where ya been, boy?" the old man asked.

Clayton stepped over Martin's body and wrapped Callie in his arms. "Are you all right?"

Callie let all the tension go and collapsed sobbing into Clayton's embrace.

"Course, she ain't *all right,* you, damned fool," the old man growled at Clayton. "Them yahoos there," he nodded toward the fallen men, "was threatenin' ta do all sorts o' mayhem ta 'er person and then was gonna tie 'er ta her bed an' burn this here store down with 'er in it, screamin'." He shrugged his shoulders and shook his gray head. "Do ya really think she'd be all right after hearin' the likes a that, boy?"

Callie sobbed into Clayton's chest. "Take 'er up ta 'er room an' get 'er dressed, boy an' I'll go for the marshal."

Several young women came barreling into the building, nearly knocking the old man to the floor.

"Oh, my god," one of the women screamed when she saw Caine's body. "What happened here?"

Mae took Callie from Clayton. "I'll help her get upstairs and get her dressed, cowboy."

CHAPTER 29

SHE'LL BE ALL RIGHT

The minutes stretched into hours, getting things sorted with Marshall Hayes and his clumsy deputies. The ungainly, nervous men stomped through her shop, knocking over dress forms, and fingering silky bloomers with their dirty hands. Callie was certain she'd seen one of them stuff several of the flimsy garments into the pockets of his trousers when he thought no one was looking.

So much for the law!

Hawk explained to Marshall Hayes about what he'd overheard in the Curly Buffalo and how he'd been coming into town to follow the men around just in case they tried anything.

He'd followed Caine and Martin from the saloon that night and watched them break into Callie's shop by way of an open window and the back door. The old man had waited outside, seen Callie and Clayton return from supper, and watched Clayton leave. When he'd heard Callie scream, he'd crept in through the open front door and listened to the men threatening her.

Hawk told the lawman he'd only shot the assailants after they'd refused to leave the building peacefully and continued to manhandle Callie. Clayton had been forced to interpret Hawk's archaic prose, but he'd been happy to do so.

The marshal and his deputies had unanimously declared the shootings justified and allowed Hawk to go on his way.

"That old man is a hell of a shot with that rifle," Marshal Hayes had said with a chuckle. "I certainly wouldn't want to be the one in his sights."

"Me neither," Clayton agreed, staring down at the bodies on the floor.

"Why do you think these two had it in for the lady?" the marshal asked. "I can believe it of that animal, Caine, but Martin ..." he said, shaking his head.

Clayton shrugged. "Martin had issues with Callie because he thought this damned shop was going to take business from him," he said, "and I guess Caine's been hankerin' after Callie since her former husband moved her into that rooming house."

The Marshal nodded. "The old man said Jamison had something to do with this plan? Where do you think he was tonight?"

"I think Evan Jamison had his hands full tonight, Marshal," Clayton said with a grin.

"Well," the Marshal said, clapping Clayton on the back, "you keep a close eye on the lady and me and my boys will keep our eyes on Jamison."

"I will," Clayton said and shook the marshal's hand. "I'll keep a real close eye on her."

❧

CALLIE WOKE the following morning stiff and sore. Her face throbbed and the thick purple welt across her belly stung. She swung her legs off the bed and ran her fingers through her hair. Chestnut strands came away in her fingers when she probed her tender scalp.

In the tidy kitchen, Callie found a pot of coffee waiting on the stove. She thanked Clayton mentally for his thoughtfulness. She poured a cup and made her way to the stairs.

I hope my stomach can handle cleaning up that mess downstairs.

At the bottom of the stairs, Callie caught the strong scent of bleach and heard the scratching of a scrub brush on wood. She peered around the corner and saw Clayton with a brush in his hand scrubbing at the gore on the wall.

"I'll clean that up," Callie scolded and stepped over a wet spot where he'd already scoured Caine's blood from the wooden floor.

Clayton turned and grinned. "Not if you were going to sleep the day away."

Callie went to the window and glanced outside. The shadows told her it must be close to noon. "You should have gotten me up." She dashed to the rolls of fabric leaning against the wall and turned each one, studying them closely for signs of blood stains. "Thank God," she sighed when she didn't find any.

"Mae and Lil were over earlier, and I told them you'd be resting today," Clayton said as he rinsed his brush in a pan of sudsy water.

"Thanks," she said. "I don't think I'm up to seeing anyone quite yet."

Clayton wiped his wet hands on his trousers and came to wrap her in his arms. "How are you feeling, Callie?" he asked and kissed the top of her head.

"I'm a little sore," she said and relaxed in his warm embrace. "Who took the bodies?" Callie asked, staring at the wet spot on the floor.

"The deputies carried 'em off to the undertakers last night," he said, turning her head away. "I suppose he notified Martin's wife this morning and ... Caine's woman was here last night."

"Oh, Lord," Callie sighed, remembering the young woman's anguished scream the night before, "Trudy."

"Who do you think will take over ownership of his brothel? Clayton asked.

Callie shrugged in his arms. "Maybe the girls will run it themselves. They've talked often enough about changes they'd make if it were theirs to run."

Clayton tipped up her chin and smiled. "Maybe now that they have a businesswoman as a friend, she can give them some pointers."

"They are all businesswomen already," Callie said. "I doubt I have much to teach any of them now that they can read and write."

"I very seriously doubt that," Clayton huffed.

Callie stepped back and took a swallow of her coffee. She stared again at the floor and walls. "Thanks again for dealing with the mess," she said and kissed his cheek. "I wasn't certain my stomach could handle it."

Clayton wrinkled his nose and creased his brow. "I almost couldn't." He picked up the bucket of dirty water. "I'll take this out and dump it, then wash out this bucket at the pump behind The Ellsworth. You can get started on all that," he said, nodding to the rolls of fabric.

As soon as Clayton left through the back door with the bucket, Callie got back to the job she'd intended the night before. She ran her hand over a roll of soft blue silk and moved it to the table where she rolled it out, gathered her patterns, pins, and sheers.

She cut through the afternoon and as darkness

closed in, Callie had blue, pink, yellow, and white sets of silk camisole and bloomer sets cut and ready to sew. She was pleased to get five sets from each bolt and saved the scrap to use for trims in the future. She cut the lengths of ribbon and lace she'd need for each set and layered them with each set of cut garments.

The next day Callie planned to sew, and she hoped Lil would come by to help her with the finish work, sewing on the tiny buttons, wrapping the buttonholes, and stringing the ribbons into the waistbands and necklines. By the end of the week, Callie hoped to have garments finished to fulfill orders taken at her opening as well as those to fill her display tables.

CHAPTER 30
THEY'RE ALL BUSINESSWOMEN

Callie and Mae stood in the shop, stocking tables and draping dress forms when something hit the window with a soggy splat, followed by another soon after.

"What the hell?" Mae gasped and rushed to the window. "You better come see this, Callie," Mae called.

"What is it?" Callie asked, walking toward the redhead, carrying a sapphire-blue dressing gown over her arm.

"There are bitches out there tossing mud at the window," Mae said with the color rising in her cheeks.

"What?" Callie said and handed Mae the dressing gown. She stormed to the window and saw globs of sloppy mud sliding down the expensive glass.

Callie flinched when another glob hit the window. This one contained some small rocks and made a clinking sound when it hit the glass.

"If they break my window, there's gonna be hell to pay," Callie hissed. "Get my gun from the back." Since the attack, Callie had purchased a Winchester rifle to keep in the back room as well as a Colt revolver she kept on her bedside table.

Callie pulled open the door and stepped out onto the wooden stoop. Four women stood in the muddy street, scooping up mud to form into balls.

"What do you think you're doing?" Callie yelled.

Amelia Martin, Carl's wife turned to glare at Callie. She stepped forward and pitched a ball of mud at the window. It missed the glass but hit the white clapboard siding of the store.

"We're covering up the filth in that window with some filth of our own," Amelia yelled back at Callie.

"That's right," another woman yelled and tossed her ball of mud.

"Our little boys are being corrupted by the filth you display in that window another woman yelled.

"Our little girls too," called the last woman Callie recognized as Vivian Hardin, Polly's mother. She tossed her ball of mud, but she didn't aim for the window. Her ball of mud hit Callie in the side of the head, and it was filled with thumb-sized rocks. Had it hit the window, Callie was certain it would have cracked or shattered the glass.

"That will be enough," Callie yelled and took a step off the porch. "Get away or …"

"Or what?" Amelia hissed. "Or you'll shoot us?" She tossed another glob of mud that hit the glass with a sloppy, wet splat.

Callie jumped when a rifle cracked behind her. "Miss Callie might not shoot ya," Mae yelled, "but I sure as hell will." She stepped beside Callie, racked the rifle, and put it to her shoulder. "Now get the hell gone," she yelled, "all y'all."

"You've got no right to threaten us, you filthy little …" Vivian didn't finish her comment because a bullet from Mae's rifle split the feathers on her bonnet and all four women ran off down the street holding their bonnets to their heads with muddy hands.

"Stupid bitches," Mae hissed, turned, and stomped back into the store.

Trudy and Tabby followed by Lil came rushing up the boardwalk from The Ellsworth House.

"Where was that flock of old crows shuffling off to?" Tabby asked.

Lil saw the mud sliding down the window and exhaled loudly, "I can guess what they were up to."

"Who was doin' the shootin'?" Trudy asked, noting Callie's empty hands.

"It was me," Mae said, stepping outside with a wet rag in her hand. "Just look what they done to Callie's window," she said pointing to the mud, "and to her," she added as she wiped mud from Callie's temple and hair.

"Are you hurt?" Lil asked as she came to Callie's side?"

"No, I'm all right," she said, brushing the fussing women aside. "I hope they didn't crack my window glass, though."

Tabby walked to the window and inspected it. "It seems to be intact," she said. "Me and Trudy will get a bucket of water and wash this mess off, Callie," she said and smiled sweetly at Callie.

"Thanks, girls," Callie said hesitantly, avoiding eye-contact with Trudy. They hadn't spoken since Caine's death. "I really appreciate it, but if you're busy next door, I can do it."

"We'll do it," Tabby said and tugged at Trudy's arm.

"You're good girls," Lil called as she urged Callie back into the store. "They'll take care of cleaning it up, sugar," she whispered, "now let's get you cleaned up."

Callie brushed a tear from her cheek. "I don't understand why people won't just leave me alone to do my business," Callie wept. "I've been careful to keep my window display decent."

"And look where that's gotten you," Lil hissed. "If it were my window, I'd fill it with corsets and frillies. Give the bitches something to really get their bloomers twisted over," she said and chuckled as she sat Callie in her chair behind the counter and used Mae's rag to clean the mud from Callie's face. "You're gonna have a bruise on your forehead," she said with a sigh.

"What's one more?" Callie said with a shrug and brushed Lil's hand away. "I'm all right."

"I know you are, sugar." She handed Callie the rag and turned to see the new dressing gown draped across the table. "You have this ready to display?"

"Yes, I was just about to put it on a dress form when Mae called me about the window."

Lil picked up the gown and smiled. "Let me and Mae dress the window today."

"Oh, my," Callie sighed, rolling her eyes. "Don't do anything that's gonna bring the Progressives down on me ... or the Baptists."

"Don't you worry none, sugar," Lil said and motioned with her bejeweled hand dismissively, "it will be discreetly suggestive, but tasteful."

Callie threw her hands up in resignation. "I'm leaving it in your capable hands, Lil." She glanced at the window where Tabby and Trudy wiped mud from the glass, smiling and waving from the outside.

"I thought Trudy would be upset with me," Callie said to Lil.

"She's tickled to be runnin' The Ellsworth," Lil

said as she wandered through the tables selecting garments for her window display.

"How's that going?" Callie asked. "Has the transition gone smoothly?"

"As smooth as silk, sugar," Lil said with a wink. "I think you can be expecting some orders for more of them fancy parlor gowns and new sets of bedding to pretty-up the rooms over there."

"That's great. Is management going to pay the bill or is it gonna fall on the individual girls?"

"Management will pick up the cost of the rooms, but the things will stay in the rooms and not travel with the girls should they go seasonal," Lil explained, "And management will make the initial outlay for the clothes and the girls will pay it back out of their takes in installments."

"Wonderful," Callie said, "I look forward to the orders."

Lil grinned. "I was in the middle of putting an order together when we heard the gunshots," she said. "I'd better get back to it so I can bring it in the morning early when I come to put this window together." She waved and walked toward the back door.

"You really gonna let that old whore dress the window?" Mae asked after they heard Lil leave.

Callie smiled and shrugged her shoulders. "I'm gonna let her give it a try.

They jumped when Clayton came rushing through the door. "What the hell happened here?" He took Callie into his arms. "The girls out front said you got hit in the head with rocks."

Damn, his arms feel so good around me.

"I'm fine," Callie said, lifting her hand to touch the tender spot on her temple. "Amelia Martin was just trying to exact a little revenge along with Vivian

Hardin and a couple of others they dragged in for moral support." She stepped away and smiled up into his handsome blue eyes. "It's nothing."

They turned when Tabby tapped on the glass. "All cleaned up, Miss Callie," the pretty young blonde said with a broad smile, waving her hand around with the dirty rag in it.

"Thank you, girls," she called and waved.

"That was real nice of 'em to clean up the mess an' all," Clayton said with his arm around Callie's shoulder.

"All the women at The Ellsworth have been a big help to me," Callie sighed and nodded to the display tables filled again with folded garments and dress forms draped in dressing gowns and newly made frocks. "I couldn't have done any of this so quickly without Lil and the girls."

"Speakin' of Lil," he said, clearing his throat.

"What about Lil?" Callie asked with an arched brow.

"I think we should treat her to a nice supper at The Flat Iron."

Callie furrowed her brow in confusion. "I agree," she said, "but I'm a bit surprised you're the one making the offer."

"She's been a big help to ya, hasn't she?"

"Yes, she has," Callie sighed, staring at the dress form with the sapphire-blue dressing gown. "She most certainly has."

"It's settled then," he said, tightening his hug around her shoulder. "We'll treat Miss Lil to a fine supper tomorrow night. I'll meet you both there at about six."

What is this man up to now?

"Will you get your old ass moving?" Clayton fussed. "I told Callie we'd meet her at six and it's near to five now."

"You should give a man warnin' when you make plans on his time, boy," Hawk grumbled as he buttoned the new wool trousers Clayton had bought for him along with a matching jacket, cotton shirt, and string tie. "I don't know what all the damned fuss is 'bout, though," he mumbled. "You plannin' ta ask that perty gal ta marry up with ya or somethin'?"

Clayton grinned. "Or somethin'," he whispered. "It's all gonna come to naught if ya don't get yourself dressed, old man," Clayton called.

It had been another long day. Callie and Lil sat together, enjoying cups of hot coffee in the café, while they waited for Clayton to arrive.

"So, what do you really think of the window display?" Lil asked as she buttered a biscuit.

Lil's display had certainly been a surprise. She'd arrived early that morning with two young men dragging a complete bed with them from the Ellsworth. The young men, who regularly came by the boarding house with wood for the stoves, had been conscripted by Lil to dismantle, carry, and re-assemble the bed in Callie's front window.

The old woman had then dressed the bed in one of Callie's bed ensembles made of a pretty bluebell print with white eyelet ruffles and bed skirt. She then placed the dress form with the blue dressing gown beside it and added a cowboy's hat and spurs to the headboard.

As promised, the display was suggestive but discreet. It added Callie's pretty bedding to her store offered inventory, as well as displaying the dressing gown *and* a set of contrasting pastel-blue camisole and bloomers Lil had added beneath the dressing gown and allowed to be glimpsed with a loosely tied sash.

"I love it," Callie gushed. "It's as promised; suggestive, but discreet."

"Should give those church bitches something to crow over for weeks to come," Lil said with an impish grin on her rouged lips.

"Indeed, it should," Callie agreed with a giggle.

"Well," Clayton said, clearing his throat uneasily, "here you are." He smiled at the two women sitting at the table. "I brought along a friend, who's been as much help to me as this fine lady has been to Callie."

Clayton pulled Hawk forward. "I'd like to introduce …"

"Daniel Hawkins?" Lil gasped and nearly dropped her coffee cup. "Is that really you?" she asked with her fingers flying to her lips as her breath caught in her throat.

The old man stepped forward, staring at the woman. "Lil? Lil Clayton?" he gasped and stared from the woman to the cowboy he'd been sharing a house with. "This is my Lil, boy," he said with tears filling his old eyes, "the one I tolt ya 'bout from Fredericksburg."

"I know, old man," Clayton said as he eased the old man into a chair between Lil and Callie. "I know."

Callie stared wide-eyed at Lil and then at Clayton.

Oh, my God. They have the same blue eyes and the same fine silver hair.

"Clayton?" Callie gasped and reached for his hand.

Lil followed Callie's eyes to the cowboy. "This is your man?" Lil asked, "Your *Clayton?*" The old woman stared intently into the cowboy's blue eyes. "Andy?" she whispered with trembling lips. "Are you really my Andy?"

"Yes, mama, it's me," he said as he glanced at Callie, "Andrew Jackson Clayton."

"Oh, sugar," the woman said and threw herself into her long-lost son's arms, sobbing, "I've been looking all over for you."

"I know, mama," Clayton said, holding the sobbing woman, "I know."

"Well, if this ain't a damned fine evenin'," the old man breathed and smiled at Callie, who sat with tears wetting her cheeks.

❧

ONCE THE TEARFUL reunion had taken place, they feasted on Mrs. Jenkins' fine fried chicken, mashed potatoes, and green beans. Lil held Hawk's hand for a while and then her son's.

"Why didn't you come to me sooner?" Lil asked.

"I wasn't certain it was you," he admitted, "until Callie told me the other day that you'd come to Kansas from Texas."

Lil's face flushed. "They called me Texas Lil."

"So, she said," Clayton said, glancing uneasily at Callie.

"I asked after you everywhere, Andy," Lil said. "I should have figured you'd have changed your name."

"I kept Clayton out of respect for my daddy," he said, and his eyes darted to Hawk. "Why'd you never tell me the truth about him, mama?"

"A boy," Lil sighed, "needed one parent he could respect, and I knew that wasn't me, so I gave you a hero father, who died at the hand of wild Indians, protecting his helpless child."

"And I thank you for that," Clayton said as he squeezed Lil's hand. "You could have thrown his cowardice in my face many times when I was being a righteous ass."

Lil grinned, "And you took your new last name after your *pony*?"

Clayton's eyes went wide. "I loved Swifty," he declared.

"I know you did, Andy," she said, patting his big hand, "I know you did." Lil turned to Hawk and smiled warmly, And what of you, Daniel? How have you spent your years since I last saw you?"

"You know me, Lil," he said with a grin on his clean-shaven face. "I wandered here an' there. I went back to Fredericksburg lookin' for ya, but they said you'd gone off lookin' for Andy." He shrugged his slumped shoulders. "I wandered and wondered after ya, but I hung on ta this," he said and took a kerchief from his pocket. "I swore I'd find ya an' return it to ya someday," he said and took Lil's hand again.

"For forty years? You've really carried this old

thing for forty years?" Lil asked as she stared at the piece of embroidered linen.

"It sounds to me like you've all been wandering and looking for someone for forty years," Callie sighed as she took a bite of peach pie.

"The question now," Hawk said as he set his coffee cup on the table "is what are we gonna do now that we all found one another?"

"I don't ..." Clayton's comment was drowned out as a boisterous crowd came rushing into the café.

"We need a table and a bottle of wine if you have one, Jenkins," Mr. Hardin called as he came into the café pushing his daughter and Evan into the room. "My little girl just got married and her new husband is buying the weddin' party supper in celebration."

Callie looked over to see Hiram and his two sons carrying shotguns behind Evan, who had a bruised lip and a huge black eye.

"Looks as though the groom mighta needed a bit o' convincin'," Hawk said with a loud chuckle.

Polly walked beside Evan and frowned at her father. Vivian, the young bride's mother, held a fretting baby in her arms as she nudged the girl along.

"The bride doesn't appear to be very happy about the situation, either," Callie said.

"That girl," Lil said, "was in The Ellsworth the other day enquiring after a room ... on the first floor," she added with a wink at Callie.

"Oh, my," Callie said, returning the old woman's grin.

Mr. Jenkins hurried ahead of the party and shoved some tables together. "Excuse me, ma'am," he said as a woman shoved past him, staring at the incoming group with tears in her big brown eyes. Callie recognized her as the new schoolteacher.

That one must have been pinning her hopes on becoming the next Mrs. Evan Jamison.

Somebody laid a hand on Callie's shoulder. Callie glanced up to see Judge Sterling grinning down at her. "I just performed the ceremony hitching those two in matrimony," he said, nodding to Evan and Polly.

When he noted Callie's hand in Clayton's his grin turned in to a smile. "Should I clear my schedule for the two of you sometime soon?" The judge walked on as the wedding party began taking their seats.

"I'm sorry," Callie said to Clayton with the color rising in her cheeks. "The judge is known to take a nip in the afternoons."

Clayton squeezed her hand and smiled. "It's actually been something weighing on my mind of late," he said and sipped his coffee.

"What's that, Andy?" Lil asked with a wide grin.

Clayton turned to his mother. "Do you think Callie would make a good daughter-in-law?"

"She'd be the best of daughters-in-law," Lil said and slapped her son's hand, "but you should be askin' her, sugar and not me."

Clayton smiled sheepishly at Callie. "How about it," he asked, "would you consider marrying up with a poor rancher now that you're a prosperous independent businesswoman?"

Callie sat staring open-mouthed at the three people grinning at her expectantly around the table.

This has got to be the lamest, most unromantic marriage proposal I've ever heard.

"Should I get up and ask Judge Sterling to come over and perform the ceremony right here and now?" Callie asked with an awkward giggle.

Hawk cleared his throat, took Lil's hand, and

blurted as he looked into the old woman's eyes, "Only if he can make it a double."

Clayton's mouth fell open.

"What?" the old man gasped. "I been waitin' forty years to make this woman my bride."

Lil stared at Hawk before turning to Callie. "What do ya say, sugar?" she asked, dabbing a tear from her eye with the dainty kerchief Hawk had carried for so long and just returned. "Shall we take these two wanderers and make proper married men out of them?"

Callie smiled and shrugged her shoulders. "I don't see why not."

CHAPTER 32

WHY NOT?

Neither woman wore white, but their dresses were beautiful. Lil wore sapphire-blue satin and Callie daffodil-yellow that brought out the red tones in her chestnut hair. Clayton and Hawk looked handsome in new black suits.

Mae stood in attendance to Callie and Trudy to Lil. Both young women were stunning in blush pink. Neither couple wanted to speak their vows in church, so Judge Sterling performed the ceremony on the shady courthouse lawn. As free food and drink were provided, most of the town showed up to witness the double ceremony.

Musicians showed up in the crowd and dancing soon commenced beneath the shade of sycamores and maples.

"It was such a pretty wedding, Callie," Mae told her when she carried over a mug of sarsaparilla from the refreshment table set up by Mr. and Mrs. Jenkins. Callie and Clayton stood beneath the shade of a maple on the courthouse lawn.

"Are you and Clayton going to be staying in the store or out at his ranch?" Mae asked as she sipped from her own mug of sarsaparilla.

"I'm thinking on a room at The Ellsworth House," Clayton teased and took a swallow of beer.

Mae rolled her eyes. "Lil said that old man is building her a house. Is that true?"

Clayton coughed beer up through his nose and Callie laughed. "It's more like Clayton doing the building while Hawk looks on giving pointers," Callie said as her eyes found the old couple cavorting with other dancers on the lawn. "Clayton gave Hawk a corner of his property and is helping him to build a little house for him and Lil."

"Awe," the pretty redhead sighed, "that's so nice."

"Would you care to dance?" Clayton's drover friend, Tom Draper, asked Mae.

"I'd be proud to," she said and took the cowboy's hand.

Clayton raised a bushy gray eyebrow and grinned. "That boy's been hankerin' after a wife for months."

Callie shook her head. "She may be good in the bedroom," Callie sighed, "but she can't cook a lick."

They watched the two younger people join the other dancers. "I seriously doubt Mae's cookin' skills are high on Draper's list of priorities in a wife," Clayton said with a chuckle.

Callie smiled and rested her head against Clayton's broad shoulder. "You're probably right," she sighed. "You're probably right.

Clayton bent and kissed the top of Callie's head. "Me and Hawk are lucky men," he sighed.

"Why is that?" Callie asked.

"We both got us women as creative in the bedroom as they are in the kitchen."

A grin spread across her face. "Indeed, you are,

Andrew Jackson Clayton, and don't you ever forget it."

"Well," someone said behind them, "this is a happy day for the both of us, Callie."

Callie turned to see Evan with a grin on his face. "Why is that, Evan? Because Polly is with child again already?"

Evan's grin disappeared. "No," he snapped, "because I no longer have to pay for your keep now that you've found a fool to do it for me."

Clayton moved Callie aside and threw a round-house punch that connected with Evan's jaw and sent him sprawling onto the grass. "That young wife of yours," Clayton said, smiling down at Evan, "seems to be very fertile. I bet she can pop out a youngin every year or so for the next ten years." He took Callie by the hand. "I hope that house of his has room to accommodate eight or ten screamin' children."

"Not nearly," Callie said, scowling down at her wide-eyed former husband. "He's gonna have to build Polly and her children a new one."

ACKNOWLEDGMENTS

I'd like to dedicate this book about a strong woman to my daughter, Tiffany Beasley Rock, another very strong woman, and an excellent storyteller.

Thank you, Dan Holmes, for all your input and editorial help. I love you.

I'd also like to say thank you to my readers. I appreciate every one of you. With that, I'd like to ask that you please go to Amazon and leave a review. Reviews are very important to us poor authors. They affect Amazon's mysterious algorithms. Thank you all!

The Grass Widow
ISBN: 978-4-86752-804-4
Mass Market

Published by
Next Chapter
1-60-20 Minami-Otsuka
170-0005 Toshima-Ku, Tokyo
+818035793528

6th August 2021

www.ingramcontent.com/pod-product-compliance
Lightning Source LLC
LaVergne TN
LVHW031431170726
843492LV00010B/2943